Five teenagers unlock the secrets of the Triangle

where the past & present collide

To: Jim

R.C. Farrington

WONDERFUL PEOPLE WHO CONTRIBUTED TO THIS BOOK:

Jason Farrington has created outstanding graphic designs
for this novel. www.farringtonstudios.com

Dale Martin and Rod Ferguson of Bermuda, have both made contributions
of their time and thoughts to help make this novel possible.

Thanks to Teddy Tucker for taking time out of his schedule to review portions
of this novel. He is a gentleman and a true pioneer in discovering,
excavating and preserving shipwreck sites in Bermuda.

ISBN: 1-894916-60-3

Production: Print Link, Bermuda
Printed in Canada

DEDICATION

This book is dedicated to the wonderful people of Bermuda, without them the true beauty of this island paradise would be lost. I would also like to dedicate this book to my family, my loving wife, Susan and sons, Gregory, Jason and Michael who have always supported my endeavors, including following me to Bermuda on an adventure of a lifetime.

BERMUDA REFERENCE BOOKS ACKNOWLEDGEMENTS:

"Bermuda Shipwrecks" *by Daniel and Denise Berg Copyright 1991*

"Hiking Bermuda 20 Nature Walks and Day Hikes"
by Cecile Davidson Copyright 2001, 2003

"Beware the Hurricane" *by Terry Tucker Copyright 1966*

"Bermuda Five Centuries" *by Rosemary Jones Copyright 2004*

"Bermuda's Architectural Heritage St. George's"
by *Bermuda National Trust Copyright 1998*

"Sailing in Bermuda" *by J.C. Arnell Copyright 1982*

ANTIQUE ART PRINTS:

Print Titled: "BLOOD MONEY ", *by Victor Nehlig*

Print Titled "VERA CRUZ", *by A.H. Payne, Dresden and Leipzig.*

Print Titled, "SANTA MARIA", *by J. Ayvasovsky.*

Print, 1917 propaganda poster of a German U-boat, by Willy Stover

Print Titled, "LANDSCAPE IN CAR-NICOBAR - VILLAGE OF SAWI".

Print titled, "HARBOUR OF ST. GEORGE'S BERMUDA, SEEN FROM SUGAR
LOAF HILL", *published in Gleason's Pictorial in 1854*

Photographs, *All photographs were taken by R.C. Farrington*

INTRODUCTION

Bermuda is the most beautiful place on earth, and whoever reads this novel should take at least one week out of their busy lives to visit one of the most incredible places on the earth. There you will find soft pristine turquoise-colored waves gently rolling up on the pink beaches. You will also find breathtaking, the myriad combinations of arbors, shrubs, vines and flowers that reflect all the colors of the rainbow. Then when you consider the historic forts, the village of St. George's and the most picturesque golf courses in the world..... Yes, Bermuda is truly an island paradise.

P.S. While you're there be sure to thank the people of Bermuda for opening up their little paradise and sharing it with you.

CHAPTERS

1. The Great Hurricane of 1780 9

2. The Tucker Cross 13

3. Tattoo Jack 17

4. The Spinners 19

5. The Adventure begins 21

6. The Smugglers 27

7. Harbour Nights 31

8. Where's the Cross? 37

9. Unfinished Cathedral - Triangle Gateway 39

10. Paradise in the Triangle...45

11. Life in the Triangle 47

12. Nazi War Mongers 51

13. Pilgrims to the Rescue 55

14. Finding Shark Hole 63

15. Signal from the triangle 69

16. Sharks and Ghost ships 75

17. Claimed For the Fatherland 81

18. The Battle of St. George's 103

19. X Marks the Spot 115

20. Finding the Emerald 125

21. Refuge in Crystal Caves 133

22. Drax Captures the Emerald...137

23. Sharks at the Gateway 147

24. Protectors of the Triangle 157

1

THE GREAT HURRICANE OF 1780

Twenty foot waves have been crashing for hours over the Spanish galleon, throwing it from side to side as the effects of the hurricane began to take its toll on the galleon. This is the worst storm in years. In fact there were more than fifty ships run ashore in Bermuda during this horrific hurricane. The rogue pirates on this ship were commanded by Captain Drax. He was one of the most evil men ever to set sail on the seven seas: his crew feared him. Drax was the type of captain who would slit your throat first, then ask questions later. He expected nothing less than one hundred percent from his men and he got it, or you were dead. The fact that they were sailing through a hurricane was proof that his crew would do anything for this evil brute, even die for him, not out of loyalty, but out of shear fear.

The galleon was sailing to Boston with the plundered bounty that they had acquired a few weeks earlier in the Caribbean. Drax had reluctantly detoured the galleon to Bermuda trying to·make safe harbour before the hurricane overtook them. It was clear to him that this one was going to be too much for the galleon to with-stand. The pirates would not be welcome in Bermuda, especially Captain Drax. He had a price on his head for murder, treason and other crimes on the high seas.

Drax was an ex British naval Lieutenant who in his younger days had murdered his frigate's Captain. The young Lieutenant James Drax lost his left ear in the saber duel that night with the frigate's Captain. After killing the Captain, he fled with the ship and it's cargo of military weapons, selling the plunder to other pirates as he sailed through the Caribbean.

Drax knows that Tobacco Bay just off the North Shore is where he can safely hide his ship and treasure until the hurricane passes. Drax tries to maneuver the ship into the tricky bay; however the ship strikes a treacherous razor sharp reef submerged beneath the boiling waves and has its underbelly ripped out. The ship is taking on water and is beginning to sink. Drax screams at the men, "Mates, get those treasure chests up to the deck and loaded into the long boats before we become bottom feeders on the ocean floor!" With that the crew scrambled to get the treasure moved to the shore as quickly as possible. Upon arriving, Captain Drax saw a cave entrance that had been uncovered in the high winds up in the rocks. "Get that treasure into the cave before we all get blown away", Drax said as he pointed towards the cave. Drax climbed up through some winding paths cut into the rocks by years of waves crashing on them so that he could better supervise the movement of the treasure to the cave.

Drax knows now that after the storm has passed. They are going to have to steal a ship from St. George's Harbour, under the cover of night, no matter what the cost is.

As the last long boat is unloaded, the full force of the hurricane strikes the Island. The storm is pounding the coastline: the wind gusts into the cave and blows over one of the treasure chests. A bright green glow emits from under the pile of gold and jewels. Drax notices this, so he reaches down and runs his fingers through the treasure until he finds the source of the glow.

"Blow me down", Drax bellowed, "Look at the size of this golden cross", it was an incredibly large solid gold cross with seven marble size green emeralds embedded on it. He picks up the hefty golden cross with bright green emeralds, but he notices that the seven emeralds appear to be drawing energy from the lightning strikes outside the cave. The cross has now formed a brilliant green laser beam in the shape of a triangle pointing towards the back of the cave causing electromagnetic explosions and green lightening blasting in all directions. Drax became enthralled with what was happening and was in a trance-like state. Never before had he ever seen such a spectacular light display.

Meanwhile a British Shore Patrol has seen the ship on the reef, has watched it break up on the rocks and sink as the hurricane grew in force. The British Lieutenant and his small patrol are helpless to investigate. They are trapped behind some large boulders on the hillside overlooking the bay. He can only view what's going on with the aid of his telescope. The eye of the hurricane now passes over the tiny Island. All is eerily calm. Lieutenant Smith commands his patrol, "Men, let's spread out and move down on the beach and surprise those pirates." The British patrol moves to the beach from their safe position on the hillside, follows the winding, rocky path up to the rock just below the cave where the pirates are now trapped. From the safe cover of a huge rock,

Lieutenant Smith yells up at the pirates, "In the King's name, drop your muskets and sabers and leave the cave. You have one minute to do so before we open fire on you". Drax hears this ultimatum and turns his head without lowering the cross, "You bloody cockroaches, here's my answer….. stick this up your royal majesty's behind". With that he signaled his first mate, Mr. Hawkins, with his free hand to commence firing at the British. The Lieutenant had no idea who he had trapped and did not expect such a quick negative response. Drax knew if he was captured it would mean the gallows for him. The only way he was going to leave the cave was over the dead bodies of the British soldiers, or dead, himself. Gunfire erupted and casualties were heavy on both sides. As the fighting continued, strange electromagnetic waves begin emitting from the cave as if a lightening storm had formed within. Captain Drax couldn't let go of the cross with all the energy pulsating through him from the cross…… his body appeared to be going through convulsions. Drax screamed, "Boys, the Devil's taking me for a ride". As the eye of the hurricane passed the full force of its winds returned. The entrance to the cave cannot withstand the strange forces from within the cave while enduring the brunt force of the immense hurricane-force winds on the outside. When the forces of nature and the forces of the unnatural collide, there is an explosion at the entrance of the cave. Drax is knocked down and the cross is hurtled outside the cave. As the opening of the cave collapses, the pirates are unknowingly drawn into the Triangle. The British solders slowly recover from being thrown down upon the rocks and beach. They move toward the smoke and debris from what used to be the entrance of the cave. Lieutenant Smith sees the cross and picks it up, then without any forewarning, he and the others are crushed and engulfed by twenty foot waves pounding on them from behind. They are swept out to sea.

In a few hours it was calm again. The hurricane had caused extensive damage throughout the Island. There was no trace of the Spanish galleon, the rogue pirates, the British Shore Patrol, or the gold and emerald cross. The Devils Triangle had struck again and concealed one of it's gateways to the world forever. It was now impossible to tell whether there ever was a cave there. The turbulent ocean settled down and the lifeless limp body of the young Lieutenant that had been washed out to sea to float for hours, finally releasing the cross from his limp hand. The Golden cross found itself drifting down to the very depths of the ocean to a ship that had been lost at sea almost two hundred years before, the Spanish galleon, the "San Pedro".

2

THE TUCKER CROSS

Years Later, 1955:

A local Bermuda treasure hunter is about to have his life changed by what he unexpectedly found on the ocean floor. Teddy Tucker had chanced upon a shipwreck just off the North Shore of Bermuda five years earlier, but had been too preoccupied with other projects to investigate the site. Today, Teddy and Robert Canton began sifting through the remains of what was left of the shipwreck. This wreck had been identified as the "San Pedro", a Spanish galleon sunk off the Devils Isles in 1595. Just beneath the surface of the ocean floor, one of the hunters found the most beautiful golden cross embedded with seven brilliant green emeralds. The cross was given the name "San Pedro Cross" although later the name was changed to the "Tucker Cross" after its recent finder, Teddy Tucker. Because the cross was found at the site of the "San Pedro", it was assumed that it had been part of the cargo on that ship. No one ever knew the real story behind the golden cross and the fact that it also served as a key to the gateways of the "Bermuda Triangle".

For many years the "Tucker Cross" was displayed at the Aquarium in Bermuda. The cross was later moved to the Bermuda Maritime Museum for a special exhibition. Soon after its arrival at the Maritime Museum at the Royal Naval Dockyard, it was discovered that the cross had been switched with a fake replica never to be seen again. The crime remains unsolved to this day. Even Scotland Yard had been called in to investigate without any success. Rumor had it that a group of local smugglers made the switch the night before the cross was to be moved to the Royal Navy Dockyard.

In 1975 the Bermuda Aquarium and Zoo did not yet have an electronic security system, so stealing such a treasure was very tempting to thieves. They just needed to be able to pick the lock on the glass case at the right time when no one else was watching. One afternoon, a group of three thieves posed as tourists and entered the Aquarium without drawing any special attention to them. A treasure collector had offered the thieves a king's ransom for the "Tucker Cross" if they could steal it. A young Bermudian by the name of Jack Skinner was picked for the team because he was an excellent picker of locks. The young thug was just launching his criminal career and this job might help him immensely in his development and notoriety. That night when the Aquarium was about to close, the three thieves found hiding places in the Aquarium until everyone had left. Skinner hid in the janitor's closet believing he was safe, however when the night janitor finished mopping the floor he took the mop and bucket to the closet. As the door began to open, Jack began to panic but because he was so slender at the time, he managed to hide behind a smock hanging on a broom in the corner of the closet. The janitor flipped open the door threw in the mop and bucket, and slammed the door shut. The janitor was in a big hurry to get to his neighbour's funeral and never noticed anything unusual.

Soon the Aquarium was empty and the thieves made their way into the room where the "Tucker Cross" was on display. Jack looked at the lock. There was nothing complicated about it so he had it unlocked in less than a minute. One of the other thieves reached in to grab the cross deftly replacing it with the cheap imitation that he was carrying in his pants pocket.

Now they had to get out of the Aquarium without anyone noticing. They slipped out a back window and crawled down to Harrington Sound which was the Eastern boundary for the entire Aquarium. They all crept quietly down into the water and headed for the Inlet, which leads into Flatt's Village. The current here was very swift this time of night because the ebb tide and full moon were causing the water to rush out of the Sound full bore as it gravitationally obeyed Newton's Law and emptied back into the ocean. Once into the Flatt's Inlet they swam frantically towards the shore where their car was hidden behind a monstrous Natal plum hedge.

It was then off to St. George's to arrange for the cross to be smuggled out of the Island from a dock location at Convict Bay. All Jack could think about on the way back was his promised fee of $5,000.00 for picking the lock. That was a small fortune for a young man back then. In their haste and carelessness, the thieves lost control of their vehicle when they made a sharp right turn off of Cut Road in St. George's onto a small winding road going down to the bottom of the cliff to Convict Bay. The car raced right through a stone wall and then it plunged into the bay, exploding into a hundred pieces, taking the passengers to "Davy Jones Locker". Jack was thrown from the car before the explosion and found himself in the waters of Convict Bay. Dazed and confused he was able to float to the surface and pull himself aboard the rusty half sunk ship, the "Typhoon" which had been in the bay for years. Young Skinner watched helplessly as the flames and wreckage sank from sight. He vowed someday to recover the cross. Jack was the only survivor from the accident that night. This was supposed to be this young Bermudian's way to get ahead, but apparently not tonight. No one ever associated the car crash with the theft of the "Tucker Cross". In fact, except for losing the cross, it was a perfect crime, no one ever knew the who, what and when about the theft.

3

TATTOO JACK

Present time:

For years Jack (Tattoo Jack) Skinner and his henchmen have been illegally collecting treasures from the 1000 plus shipwrecks around Bermuda. He's been illegally selling these artifacts to collectors all over the world. By doing so he has been cheating the Government of Bermuda out of the 50 percent tax on artifacts and treasures that are found in Bermuda's territorial waters. In fact many of these finds should be displayed in local Bermuda museums to preserve the Bermuda heritage for Bermudians and tourists to enjoy. Tattoo is still looking for the big jackpot. He, as do many local Islanders, believes that over 200 years ago an unknown stolen Spanish galleon was wrecked on the reefs off the North Shore of Bermuda and that before the galleon sank the pirate crew was able to move most of the treasure to an unknown location on Bermuda. To date no one has been able to find any trace of that treasure. On another note, over the years, Tattoo Jack had on many occasions sent his team of divers down to the wreckage of the car from that fateful night years ago at the bottom of Convict Bay to find the "Tucker Cross", but to no avail.

Tattoo Jack operates a deep sea sport fishing operation which is really a front for his illegal treasure smuggling ring. He takes fake clients, (who are really treasure collectors) out to sea twenty to thirty miles offshore and meets up with their small vessels who accept his stolen artifacts from him after paying him handsomely for them. These yachts then sail to the east coast of the US or south to the Caribbean with their treasures. Tattoo Jack will even accept any illegal cargo to bring back to Bermuda, guns, drugs it doesn't matter. Although the local law enforcement agencies believe Tattoo Jack is in some type of illegal activities they have yet to be able to prove anything.

The Shinbone Pub located in the Shinbone Alley, it's a local pub and the main hangout for Tattoo Jack and his henchmen. His trusted thugs are Cuda, Sledge, Gunner and Axle.

4

THE SPINNERS

Michael Clark is deep in thought as he stares out the Delta 757 jet's window. All he sees are blue skies, a few white puffy clouds, and beautiful blue water as far as the eye can see. He is on his annual summer trip to Bermuda to stay with his grandmother in St. George's for the summer. He'll miss his home in Boston, but not for long. He can't wait to see all his friends he has not seen since last summer. Michael wonders how the year has changed them. He just turned 15 and is anxious to see how much his friends have grown. He does have a surprise for all of them......his parents had made for them special sterling silver key chains with a triangle connected to the chain engraved with the word "Spinners". The triangle has a spinner connecting the top of the triangle to the chain, thus it spins. This is the perfect symbol for the group that calls themselves "Spinners", meaning "tall tales or adventures". The airport is at the same end of the Island as St. George's, so he hopes his friends will be there to meet him.

Keno Ming is dark skinned and is very large and powerful for his 15 years. He lives at the St. David's Lighthouse where his father is the lighthouse keeper.

Samantha (Sam) Savage is a beautiful and brilliant young girl. She is 14 years old and is considered the "brains" of the group. Her father is Inspector Ian Savage, a local police Inspector for the St. George's branch of the Bermuda Police Force.

Roderick (Portagee) Madeiros is the "little" and the youngest at 13 years old, but an "inventive" Portuguese boy who is an electronic whiz kid.

Graham Aston is dark skinned and also 15 years old. He is the "rich" kid of the group. His family is the dominant oil importer in Bermuda.

The pilot breaks Michael's trance with an announcement from the flight deck. "This is Captain Gregory James and on behalf of the crew and myself I would like to welcome you to Bermuda.

For those of you seating on the left side of the plane you can see St. George's off in the distance". When Michael looked out and saw the village he loved to call his second home, he lost the sound of the Captain's voice and began to envision his destination. St. George's is small village at the east end of the Island. The village is hilly with small winding streets that remind you of a small European village. The village provides Michael and his friends with an endless playground of historic sites to explore. There are forts, the historic Unfinished Cathedral, several beaches, and the business district of the village.

As Michael had hoped, his friends were there waiting for him as he left the confines of the airport. To his amazement everyone still looked the same, maybe a little taller, and yes Sam was even prettier. Tomorrow Michael and his friends, "The Spinners", will be off and running, seeking the next big adventure. This is where "The Lost Treasure of Bermuda" adventure begins.

5

THE ADVENTURE BEGINS

The Spinners are in that age group of teenagers being too young to drive and too old to want their parents to take them anywhere. At 16 you can get a driver's license to drive a 50 cc scooter and at 18 you can drive a car. Next summer some of them will be able to drive a scooter, but until then most of their time will be spent in St. George's with the occasional bus trip to Hamilton or the South Shore beaches. The kids spend lots of time goofing off around St. George's. They also play video games at each other's houses. On clear days they also have a couple of beaches to go to, but their best times are the time they spend treasure-hunting around the old forts and remote shorelines on the North Shore.

The big excitement each week of the summer is the Tuesday night "Harbour Nights". The village is full of excitement on these evenings because the docking cruise ships always have hundreds of tourists visiting. All the stores are open, there are street vendors selling their souvenirs, and plenty of local cuisine to sample. Some "Harbour Nights" the kids like to take their punt, (row boat) out to Convict Bay to the "Typhoon", a half sunk shipwreck. Once aboard the old rusting scrub bucket they hide and watch the activities in the village square and later the fire works show that sometimes accompanies "Harbour Nights".

The Spinners do have a couple of old, but working metal detectors. Miraculously

Portagee manages to keep the detectors working. Anyone else would have long thrown them away. Depending where they search, they find everything from coins and jewelry to bottle caps and beer tabs. In the early evening hours they search the beaches, which provide them with spending money from the lost coins they find in the sand. For treasure items, they search around the old forts and cliffs, but alas, to date, they have only found old bike parts, bottles, a few old coins and lots of junk. However they all know that some day they'll find a treasure chest full of Spanish doubloons, pearls and jewelry worth a fortune.

Today the Spinners head to the Unfinished Cathedral to see what riches await them. Its late afternoon, so the kids want to make sure no one sees them entering the ruins. The church is off limits and deemed not safe for tourist or local residents to enter. Once inside, however, it's hard for anyone on the outside to see them. The metal detectors are quickly turned on, and as expected, their gauges go berserk and the loud crackling in their headsets is too much to bear. For years electromagnetic anomalies and strange magnetic fields around the Unfinished Cathedral have been detected, however no one has been able to give a logical explanation. In the 1870's when the new Cathedral was being constructed, there were many unexplained phenomenon around the site. Construction progress was severely compromised. In fact, after years of construction the site was abandoned and the Unfinished Cathedral just sits there slowing crumbling away through the ages. Portagee has also detected similar, but weaker electromagnetic and magnetic fields at Shark Hole. He thinks the signals might be weaker because they are partially beneath the water. This is a local cave that is half submerged in water. At times sharks enter the opening of the cave to feed. Portagee, being the electronic whiz kid that he is, wonders if these conditions have something to do with the Bermuda Triangle. So without the aid of their detectors the kids make the best of it. They crawl around on their hands and knees digging through the sand and rocks with their small garden shovels. Sam is trying a new tool today. She had borrowed a flour sifter from her mom's kitchen. She plans to use it to sift through the sand. She reckons she could get through a lot more material quickly with the sifter. After about an hour and half after finding just some old square nails, a few coins and some old beer cans the kids decide its time to head home for supper. Sam's sifter worked great, but Graham wonders if Sam's mom might notice that the sifter may not quite be the same any more. Sam says "I've never seen her use it. I think it came from my granny's kitchen years ago".

Once back in the village the Spinners head their separate ways. Keno headed for the bus station since the walk back to the lighthouse would be too tiring tonight. Sam went over to Michael's house to have dinner with him and his grandmother and Graham is supposed to meet his parents at one of the local restaurants to have dinner with them. Oh and of course Portagee is heading to the harbour to see what his father had brought after the day's fishing trip. While Portagee is waiting on the dock he sees Tattoo Jack come cruising into the harbour in his big expensive deep sea fishing boat, the "Black Shark".

They docked, tied up the boat and then as anybody would expect, you reckoned you would see them bringing out their catch of the day, but no. Instead he sees Sledge and Gunner struggling with a large lumpy and apparently heavy duffel bag. Tattoo Jack is right behind them and yells at them: "you idiots hurry up and get that into the back of the pickup before I kick your butts". They quickly do his bidding and head off to the Shinbone Pub for their nightly round of drinks. Axle was left behind mumbling to himself, because he always has to lock down the "Black Shark". He will join his fellow goons later. Portagee's father is late, which happens a lot, so out of curiosity Portagee runs down the narrow streets taking a couple of shortcuts to Shinbone Alley. As he suspected the group were already in the pub gulping down their ale and rum. No one was watching the truck……..after all who would be stupid enough to mess with Tattoo Jack's property. The temptation was too much for Portagee. He climbed in under the canvas door at the back of the truck. Once in he sees the large bag, he feels around it, he can tell there are many different objects of different sizes and shapes. Portagee unsnaps the bag and peeks in but it's so dark in the truck he can't see anything. In frustration, he tries to dump the bag out a little and "bang, boom", shipwreck artifacts spill out all over the back of the truck. Shocked, Portagee sits there and stares at the treasure, totally forgetting how much noise he had caused. Meanwhile the noise was heard from inside the pub. Tattoo Jack says "Sledge! Get your butt out there and see what that boom was". Sledge nods his head dazedly as he's in a slightly drunken stupor and he staggers for the door. His problem was that he had been drinking before they left the "Black Shark".

Sledge looks around outside, doesn't see anything, not that he would anyway in his condition but then he decides to look in the back of the truck. He flips back the canvas, and sees the mess and a black outline of a person and yells: "hey mate, what the hell are you doing in my truck?" Portagee almost jumps out of his skin from fright, but he quickly recovers and throws a small brass ships bell at Sledge hitting him in the forehead. Sledge falls backwards out of the truck hitting the back of his head on the hard brick street. While Sledge is screaming and cursing bloody murder, Portagee jumps out of the truck, but just before he jumped he instinctively picked up a small gold coin that was glinting on the truck bed. In his hurry he lands right smack in the middle of Sledge's fat beer belly, causing a few more earth-shattering expletives. Portagee quickly picks himself up and runs as quickly as he can down the narrow street looking for the first alley to turn into. By now, Jack and his men have rushed out of the pub door to see Sledge struggling to his feet. Then out of the corner of his eye, he sees a small figure running down the alley. Jack screams "Gunner get this mess in the truck cleaned up, Cuda you follow that boy". Cuda runs after the dark shadow, as Portagee turns the corner at full speed. Then he looks up and sees Axle right in front of him on his way to the pub from the "Black Shark". Portagee quickly side-steps him and moves on at full stride. Axle turns around to see what blur just passed him but soon continues strolling along in the direction of the pub "BAMB". Cuda ran into him at full speed. Both goons are sprawled out on the alley dazed and bleeding from the crack on their sculls. By now,

Tattoo Jack is on the scene and just barely sees Portagee round another corner just out of sight. Jack yells: "you little thief when I catch up to you, you won't even make good shark bait". As Jacks turns around he looks down and sees a small keychain in the shape of a triangle. He picks it up and says: "I think I can find my little thief now".

The next morning the Spinners meet where they do every day, at the end of Blacksmith's Hill Street. This is one of the secondary entrances to St. George's where the kids can meet and not be noticed by others. Portagee is beside himself, very nervous and chanting in Portuguese which no one else can understand. Sam puts her arm around him, trying to calm him down and asks, "Roderick, what's the matter? Did the bullies from school give you a hard time again?" Portagee just shrugged. Keno chimed in "brother, I'm here for you, waz-up?" Michael and Graham just stood there in silence not sure what to say or do. "Is it a problem at home?" Sam asked. Finally, almost in tears, Portagee with trembling lips spoke, "last night while I was waiting for my father down at the harbour….". Portagee then told the group what had happened the night before. All the rest of the Spinners were amazed to hear what happened. Keno said" let's go back down to the Shinbone Pub and kick Tattoo Jack's butt". Graham said, "Are you nuts? …… they'll take us out in the harbour and drown us". Michael suggested a real wimpy path. "Why do anything? … they never would have got a good look at you anyway". Portagee looked a little ill, then gulped and said "they will figure it out sooner or later. What I forgot to tell you was that last night I lost my Spinner keychain there in front of the Shinbone Pub. I bet they'll find it and start asking about the "Spinners". Sooner or later they'll figure out it was one of us". Sam responded, "Maybe we should take the gold coin and show my dad?"

Everyone agreed that that was the best thing to do. So they headed down York Street to the St. George's police station. As the Spinners turned the corner, Inspector Savage was just heading out the station door. Surprised by seeing Sam and the boys, he stopped and said, "What are you kids up to this morning ….. breaking any laws?" Michael said without thinking, "Yeh, pull out you gun and arrest us". Inspector Savage smiled, and then pulled open his blazer with no sign of any weapon: "remember Michael, guns are banned in Bermuda. Not even police officers use them on a daily basis….. we have to be really good here", the Inspector said. Michael was a little embarrassed and his face notched up a few shades of red. "Dad", Sam said and began to tell her father the story as Portagee had related it earlier. Inspector Savage listened intently then politely posited: "Is this really true? Or are you kids just spinning another tall tale?" The Spinners all assured him they were telling the truth, or at least what Portagee had told them, but they could sense the Inspector was still a little skeptical.

Then Portagee remembered the gold doubloon in his pocket. "Inspector sir", exclaimed Portagee, "here's the gold doubloon that was in the back of their truck". The Inspector queried: "Are you sure that's where you found it?" "Yes sir", replied Portagee. "Well done", the Inspector replied, "You kids go off and keep out of mischief and stay away from the harbour. I'll pay Mr. Skinner a little visit before he heads out on his boat this morning". The Spinners decided it was best to leave the downtown area of St. George's and head to the beach at Tobacco Bay for a change.

Meanwhile Inspector Savage walked down to the harbour and waited for Tattoo Jack to show up. While he waited, he wondered if the whole story was really true. Maybe he might finally be able to bring Tattoo Jack to justice for some of the crimes he knew he suspected he was guilty of. After waiting for about twenty-five minutes, the Inspector heard the out-of-tune engine of Tattoo Jack's flatbed pulling up next to his fishing boat. As Jack and his thugs approached, the Inspector took the Doubloon from his pocket and flipped it to Tattoo Jack and saying, "Mr. Skinner, aren't you missing your coin?" Tattoo glanced at the coin and quickly replied, "Why Inspector Savage, I collect fish not coins", "Well then Mr. Skinner, would you mind if I take a gander at the flatbed of your truck and your boat?" "You got a search warrant?" asked Tattoo. "No, but I could have one here in a forty minutes, so it's your choice. Mr. Skinner, what will it be?" Tattoo Jack reluctantly replied, "O.K. Go ahead Inspector". As the Inspector lifted the canvas on the back of the truck, Tattoo Jack leaned over to Sledge and whispered, "If he finds anything club him and we'll dump him twenty miles out to sea". But curiously enough, after the Inspector searched both the truck and the boat he came up with nothing incriminating. The Inspector told Tattoo Jack that nothing was found, but he would be keeping a weather eye on his activities. Tattoo Jack replied as the Inspector walked off, "When I get done with you, you'll be pounding a beat again flatfoot!"

6

THE SMUGGLERS

A couple of days later, Tattoo Jack and his thugs met at the Shinbone for their breakfast of codfish and potatoes. After the surprise visit by Inspector Savage, Tattoo needed to be more careful with his smuggling business until the heat was off. Because of his intimidating tactics with the locals, he had never before had a problem with anyone ratting on him. Tattoo cautioned his thugs: "Sooner or later, we are going to find the snitch who squealed on us. I'll bet it's the brat who lost this damn key-chain". He held it in his hand absent-mindedly spinning the triangle in his hand. Then his eyes lit up as he stopped the twirling keychain and read the inscription. "Spinners", He says: "What do you mates think this means? No one answered….. they were all too busy stuffing their faces. Tattoo saw their disinterest and slammed his hand down on the table as hard as he could as he yelled, "What in the hell does Spinners mean?"

Cuda choked on a potato and spit it on the floor. Axle was leaning back on his chair half asleep. The bang startled him and he fell over backwards hitting his head on the wood floor with an amazingly solid thump. Sledge and Gunner started laughing, but this only made matters worse. Tattoo reached over and cracked both of their heads together threatening, "If you think that's so damn funny I'm going to spin your butts down to the bottom of the ocean with hundred pound anchors chained to your legs. Now, let's get real… what does Spinners mean?" Finally Sledge said, "I think it's a gang of some little rich kids here in St. George's, maybe even the daughter of the Inspector". Tattoo Jack had a nasty-looking smirk on his face and said, "Well, this is starting to make a bit of sense now, there is a connection here. Alright, let's get down to business".

Everybody decided to smarten up....Tattoo Jack wasn't kidding.

That day they were scheduled to deliver a load of illegal artifacts to a Brazilian collector who had been waiting for several days about thirty miles off the south coast of Bermuda. "Cuda and Sledge, you two need to get the "Black Shark" ready. This is gonna be a tough trip. We'll be out for a couple of days at least, but at least the weather looks promising. We'll try to sneak back tomorrow night under the cover of darkness, so we won't have to explain where our bloody fish catch is. Make sure you have provisions for us plus loads of black rum". He then turned to the other two, "You two idiots load up the truck at the warehouse with the merchandise and drive the truck over to Tobacco Bay". This was on the back side of the Island and if the Inspector was watching the "Black Shark" it would appear that they were leaving the harbour on a run of the mill deep-sea fishing trip. Once out of sight of land they would double back to Tobacco Bay and connect with Axle and Gunner with their truckload of merchandise. Gunner would then board the "Black Shark" and Axle would return the truck to the warehouse. Axle would then rendezvous with the "Black Shark" on their trip the following night. The plans went according to plan, by noon they were heading south of the Island. It would not be until the next morning that they would pull alongside the Brazilian yacht. That night they sat around the "Black Shark" drinking rum and smoking their Cuban cigars. Tattoo Jack was still playing with the Spinner keychain in his hand, flicking it repeatedly with his fingers. It had become a fixation...an obsession. He just couldn't get it off his mind. As the hours went on, sobriety began to dissolve, weird thoughts confused their brain cells and like clockwork, one by one, they passed out in the smoky cabin.

"HHHHHHMMMMMMMMMMMMMMMMMMMM", the ear numbing sound of an air horn assaulted Tattoo Jack's ears as he just about suffered his first cardiac. His first fear was that the "Black Shark" had drifted back towards Bermuda and that they were about to be boarded by the Bermuda Harbour Police. Instead, as the mental fuzziness and blurred vision began to correct to normalcy, he could see it was the Hermanos de Brazil. The Brazilians hated being called that because they thought the Bermudians were a bunch of small time thieves and thugs. As the two boats tied up, Tattoo called: "How was the trip for the Hermanos de Brazil", Alvaro the Captain of the yacht, "Piranha", shouted back: "One more smartass comment out from your sorry ass and this Piranha will send you and your worthless crew to the bottom of the ocean". Tattoo knew he had come treacherously close to going too far with the Brazilians and it was time to get serious. "Boss Man", said Tattoo, "Are you ready to inspect and load your cargo?". Alvaro was impatient after hovering for three days in lumpy seas to get this over with so the cargo transferring from the "Black Shark" to the "Piranha" began. Alvaro was impressed with the quality of the merchandise, and he tossed a heavy briefcase over to

Tattoo. Tattoo smiled then opened the case. The sight of the $100,000.00 in small US notes was intoxicating. Alvaro yelled to his crew, "Free the lines….. it's time to head home"; Tattoo grabbed one of the ropes and said, "Whoa Mate, aren't you forgetting something?" Alvaro looked surprised, but he really knew what Tattoo Jack was wanting. Alvaro turned around to his crew and said, "Right, let's give these worthless Bermudians their other package". Two crew members threw over a 50 kilo bail of cannabis which Tattoo could make a quick profit on when back in Bermuda. The two exchanged farewells and went off separate directions. With the 50 kilo cargo of cannabis, Tattoo would definitely have to enter St. George's Harbour after dark. In fact tonight would be perfect…….. it was "Harbour Nights" in St. George's. There would be a cruise ship taking up most of the dock, the Customs officials would be preoccupied with honeymooners disembarking the ship and to top it off there might be a fireworks show as well to make the shadow their demure return.

Tattoo Jack sat back with his Cuban cigar in one hand and his glass of Dark N Stormy in the other as he slowly motored back toward Bermuda.

7

HARBOUR NIGHTS

The afternoon was pretty well spent when the Spinners headed to town for Harbour Nights. Sam could not go tonight as her father was on duty and her mom was off the Island for a week or more, therefore Sam had to stay home and baby-sit her little sister. There was a cruise ship docked at the Harbour tonight with over 2000 tourists aboard. Tonight was going to be a big night, a huge fireworks display had indeed been planned for the evening. The big events were hours away, but the Spinners had different plans. They headed down to the dock and all climbed into Portagee's family punt.

They rowed out to their favourite shipwreck in Convict Bay, the "Typhoon". It was going to be an unusually late afternoon of swimming, diving and snorkeling off the "Typhoon". The kids tied up the punt on the landside of the wreck. The old wreck was covered with rust and jagged edges, so the kids had to be very careful. They all had their swimsuits on under their clothes. They dropped their shorts, tossed off shirts, discarded shoes and threw all their "stuff" on the punt. It had been a great afternoon. Everybody was having a ball doing their own thing. Michael and Graham were snorkeling while Keno and Portagee were taking turns diving off the wreck. This was the first time the kids had gone snorkeling around the wreck since Hurricane Fabian hit the Island the year before. It was a no-brainer that the old wrecks and the floor of the bay had been

drastically altered by the hurricane's wave action. Michael and Graham were having a great time looking at the new scenery Mother Nature had transmogrified. Michael was pawing frantically through some of the debris on the bottom when he noticed something very bright out of the corner of his eye. At first, he thought it was just another old beer can and almost didn't give it another thought. Then a shimmering Sergeant Major swam in the same direction as the shiny glimmer. Michael then noticed that the glint was golden and much brighter than the pedestrian yellow on the adult Sergeant Major. Michael suddenly realized that he was snorkeling and not scuba diving. He was almost out of air and he needed to surge up to the dancing bluish-white surface. As he panicked upwards, he managed to tap on Graham's shoulder and pointed up. Graham nodded and followed Michael to the surface. When they surfaced Michael gasped in excitement and started trying to talk to Graham with the snorkel still planted in his mouth. Graham reached over and pulled the snorkel out of Michael's mouth and said, "Michael, slow down. Start over, what are you trying to tell me?" Michael took a breath and said: "I wouldn't swear on a stack of Bibles, but I think I saw something that could be jewelry down there. Are you ready to go back down to double check?" Graham nodded and they both dove back down to the bottom of the bay.

It took a few seconds but Michael was able to find the glimmering object again. He reached down and touched the part of the object that was exposed - it was gold and appeared to be very thick. Michael then brushed away the remaining silt and sand.

"Oh my God", Michael thought, "It's a golden cross decorated with seven marble-size green emeralds'.

Michael picked the cross up and headed towards the surface. Graham appeared to be in shock and just stared. But his trance was interrupted when his brain screamed out for some fresh oxygen, so he rushed to the surface. Once on the surface both boys climbed on board the wreck and called the others over to see what Michael had discovered.

When everyone was there Michael said, "Look at this cross. It's gotta be worth a fortune."

Keno could not believe what he was looking at.

"Guys, it's the Tucker Cross. It's stolen property. It's been missing for 30 years."

Graham said, "Maybe there's a finder's fee or reward for it."

All the others agreed that this would be the fairest way to deal with the find. As it was getting dark now, the kids thought it was a good time to dry off and get dressed. They had brought snacks so they could sit down and relax leaning against the outboard of the hull of the wreck that gave them a commanding view of the shore. This way they could monitor all the activity at the town square where the cruise ship was docked and they would get a spectacular view of the fireworks display. As it turned dark the Spinners munched on their snacks absent-mindedly, observed the activities and talked about the Tucker Cross.

Axle was now rowing his punt to the designated rendezvous site to signal the "Black Shark" that it was safe to enter the bay. As Axle got closer to the wreck he overheard voices on board. He stopped to listen and after a while he figured that the kids had found the "Tucker Cross" and that they had it with them on board the wreck. Axle, not being too smart, still rationalized that he should row out 100 yards further into the bay so he could tell Tattoo Jack what he had heard without alerting the kids. Soon the "Black Shark" entered the bay. Axle saw the boat heading dead straight towards his tiny punt and he started yelling at them to veer off. The Spinners heard the commotion and looked behind them to see the "Black Shark" looming towards them. No one on the "Black Shark" saw or heard Axle. In fact they were not even looking for him yet and with the engine sputtering away they couldn't hear his screams.

Keno now saw Axle in the punt and said, "He must have been listening to us and is trying to warn Tattoo Jack. Let's get out of here before it's too late."

Everyone agreed and quietly slipped over the gun whale of the wreck into the punt and paddled to shore as quietly as they could.

But it was too late for Axle. The "Black Shark" split his punt in two. The sudden jar aboard the "Black Shark" and Axle's screams caused Sledge to kill the engines. Gunner and Cuda ran to the boat's bow to see what they had struck.

Looking down Sledge said, "Stop. It's Axle in the water, we just ran over him."

Sledge and Gunner threw Axle a line and pulled him up onto the boat. Tattoo now came forward and was "steaming mad".

"What the hell is the matter with you Axle? You were supposed to signal us from in front of the "Typhoon" if it was safe to enter the harbour."

Axle said, "Yes, but I know where the Tucker Cross is."

Tattoo Jack stopped dead in his tracks….. all ears. Axle went on and told what he had overheard from the kids on the wreck. Tattoo Jack had the searchlights trained on the wreck and idled up to its side. To his disappointment no one was there. However, in the haste of rushing away the kids had left their tracks, so he knew Axle was telling the truth. Tattoo now knew the Spinners were 4 or 5 kids, that they had his cross, and he would resort to anything to get the Tucker Cross back.

The fireworks show was well underway now. Tattoo turned to his crew and said, "Mateys, let's get this show on the road. Axle you're one too many for our official crew. If we were being watched you didn't go out to sea with us so you better not dock with us either. Inflate the rubber raft and head ashore. Take this case of money with you too. We'll meet you at the Shinbone."

Axle inflated the raft, threw it overboard and started rowing for the shore. Cuda restarted the engine on the "Black Shark". They were now ready, under the cover of darkness and the distraction of the fireworks, to quietly approach the docks.

Tonight Inspector Savage was on duty at "Harbour Nights". He also had a team of (undercover) officers who were mingling in the crowd around the village square. As expected, the crowd was large and there were lots of street vendors. The Inspector knew that the "Black Shark" had set out on a fishing trip two days ago and had not yet returned. He kept glancing towards the docks to see if they might return tonight. Lo and behold, just as he was thinking about the "Black Shark" along it came, engines off just coasting towards the docks. The Inspector pulled out his police radio and called for support. "Officers Gregory and John meet me ASAP down at the docks. The Black Shark has pulled alongside."

By the time Inspector Savage arrived Sledge and Cuda were just swinging the 50 kilo bail to throw it off the boat and onto the dock. At that very moment Tattoo saw the Inspector approaching and yelled, "Stop! Get that bail over to the other side of the boat and throw it overboard."

Seeing what was going on, Savage now in a dead run for the boat yelled back: "This is the Police. Drop that bail now!"

The other two officers were now also on the scene and jumped onto the "Black Shark". A scuffle ensued. Tattoo's men were trying to toss the bail overboard and the officers were trying to intervene. The scuffle ended as quickly as it had started when

Officer Gregory struck Cuda in the back with his night stick. The bail was dropped and Cuda and Sledge stuck up their hands. Tattoo was sweating bullets realizing the fact that he was about to be arrested with 50 kilos of cannabis. The officers picked up the bail and heaved it onto the dock. Savage was now trying to be very circumspect with this unexpected drug bust. He didn't want to do anything that might let Skinner get off the hook.

He said, "Skinner you and your crew sit down on the boat's deck and keep your mouths shut."

He then looked at the officers and said, "Officer Gregory you stay on board and watch our friends. Officer John, you come with me and let's examine this bail."

Officer John reached over and cut the top of the bail open. Officer John and the Inspector just stood there staring at the contents of the bail for a minute without uttering a word.

The Inspector finally spoke. "Officer please go down to the cruise ship and bring back one of the Customs Officers. Skinner do you have anything to say about your cargo before Customs arrive?"

Tattoo just looked at Savage as if looks could kill. Then he said, "Yeah, why don't you take that bail and stick it up your ass?"

Savage smiled and decided to wait for Customs before saying anything further. Finally, the Customs Officer showed up with Officer John.

Savage turned to the Customs Officer and said: "Officer, Mr. Skinner has intentionally tried to smuggle into Bermuda a bail of horse food and he also has tried to evade paying duty on such goods. It is illegal to bring into Bermuda non inspected hay. Officer, please charge this man accordingly."

Then turned to his Officers and waved them off, "Come on Officers let's get back to the fireworks show."

As he turned away, Inspector Savage had a smirk on his face from ear to ear. He did wish however, he could have busted Tattoo on the drug charge "Importing with the intent to distribute". Meanwhile, Tattoo was left standing there in a serious jumble of mixed emotions. First, he was relieved that he wasn't facing a jail term of twenty years. Secondly, he was furious with Inspector Salvage for making him look like a dunce and thirdly he wanted to kill Alvaro for double crossing him. Now he had to sit there while a Customs officer wrote him up.

Tomorrow is another day, Tattoo thought. Now it was time to recover the Tucker Cross.

8

WHERE'S THE CROSS?

The Spinners left "Harbour Nights" as quickly as possible. They went directly to Graham's house as this was probably the safest place to be while they decided what to do. The guys felt safe there, at least for now. Graham's house, or his compound as one might describe it, was totally surrounded by native limestone walls eight feet high with electronic iron gates at the entrance. The games room is one of the rooms that no one ever visited except Graham and his friends.

As the guys settled down in their favourite chairs, Keno started: "Listen up guys; we have to figure this out. Tattoo Jack either already knows who we are or soon will and he knows we have the Tucker Cross."

"We need to get hold of Sam in the morning and have her dad help us turn it into the authorities," Michael said.

Portagee being a little nervous said, "I don't think it's safe for us to be out on the streets tonight. Graham would it be OK with your parents if we spent the night?"

"No problem," replied Graham. "Go call your parents and let them know."

They all called their homes to make sure their parents and grandparents approved. The rest of the evening was spent playing video games. This helped relax the boys and get their minds off Tattoo Jack. Tomorrow they would meet with Sam and her dad.

Tattoo Jack and his crew left the "Black Shark" and met up with Axle at the Shinbone Pub to discuss the day's events and plan their next moves. Tattoo Jack was still so pissed off he couldn't see straight.

"How could this night have gone so bad?" Tattoo exclaimed. "First we lost the cross, and then we were duped with phony cannabis, almost arrested and then embarrassed by Inspector Flatfoot. Alright, let's forget about the cannabis, we'll nail Alvaro later. The Tucker Cross is what I want. It's mine and I want it back." He then pounded on the table repeatedly. "Tomorrow each of you take your walkie talkies with you and spread out over the village. You've gotta keep at it 'til you find those kids."

Tattoo knew that the cross would now bring him over a million dollars. He was so close to it he could taste it.

"If that cross leaves St. George's tomorrow I will have someone's head, is that bloody-well understood?"

All nodded submissively.

Tattoo stood up and headed for the pub door, "Good night mates. Get some rest. I don't want any mistakes tomorrow." Tattoo then slammed the door behind him.

9

Unfinished Cathedral - Triangle Gateway

Sam was awakened this morning by thunder, which was a little unusual for Bermuda. It looked like today was going to be a gloomy rainy day. She heard her dad already moving around the house, getting ready for work. Before Sam could get up, her dad came into the room.

"Morning Sam," he said. "I'll be in Hamilton all day today at court. My cell phone will be off so I'll catch up with you tonight."

He then gave her a hug and a kiss and headed out of the door.

Sam waved and said, "Love you dad, bye."

He replied, "Bye, love you too."

An hour later Sam's cell phone rang, Sam picked it up and she sees Michael's caller I D.

"Morning, Mikey, how was Harbour Nights last night?"

Michael responded, "That's what I'm calling about. We're in deep trouble and need help…..big time!" He then went on and told Sam the story.

"Sam, we need to show your dad the cross and have him help us."

Sam replied, "That's impossible daddy's in court all day in Hamilton and he won't be home until late tonight."

"Can well call him?" Michael asked.

"No, his cell is always turned off when he has Court Duty," Sam replied.

"Well then, what can we do?" Michael asked.

"Let me meet you guys over at Graham's and we'll take it from there."

"OK, see ya!" Michael replied.

"See ya!" Sam said.

Sam finished dressing, put on her rain suit and headed out the front door. She made a beeline for Graham's house. More dark clouds were rolling in offshore, the rain was pouring down in diagonal sheets - the type of rain you have to keep your head down just trying to keep your eyes from stinging with the raindrops. It was a long hike to Graham's house. She headed for the village town square. When she entered the square, Cuda spotted her from inside the doorway of a tourist shop. Sam, head down, was paying more attention to the puddles in the brick pavers than her surroundings and who was watching her. After she passed by Cuda, he called out on the walkie talkie,

"Mates, the Inspectors daughter just walked across the square and are going up Water Street. I'm sure she is one of the Spinners. Will follow her?"

The others acknowledged and they would all start moving into the village area.

Sam now turned right, going right by the police station. Cuda got a little nervous thinking she was going to the police station to see her dad. To his pleasant surprise she walked by the station and on up to York Street. When crossing York Street she did finally notice one of Tattoo goons, it was Axle trying to hide by the bus station. She now knew she was being followed. Sam quickly went up Ocean Street. It's a pretty long and slightly winding residential street, with lots of places to make a quick exit. Half way up the street Sam slipped through a gate, shot around to the back of the small cottage, then crawled under the Oleander bushes in the back yard and was gone. By now both Cuda and Axle were on a dead run up Ocean Street. A couple of hundred yards up the street they stopped, panting, looking around, and nothing. Both knew they had been ditched.

Cuda called out on the walkie talkie, "We lost the girl on Ocean Street, and anyone else sees her?"

There was no response from anyone.

Then all of a sudden Tattoo blares out, "You idiots better find her quickly."

All went silent again.

Sam finally made it to Graham's house just as the gale force winds from the storm picked up. She pressed the intercom button on the gate to let Graham know she was there. He opened the automatic gate from the games room. Sam walked around to the back of the house and knocked on the back door to the games room. Portagee opened the door and before he could say anything Sam almost knocked him down rushing inside. She was very nervous and scared. After sitting down for a minute she told them what had happened on her way. Meanwhile, lurking behind some shrubs just outside the gate of Graham's house was Gunner, who just by luck saw Sam enter the gate at the last moment. He called Tattoo on the walkie talkie seeking instructions. Tattoo told him to stay there to keep tabs on them and let him know if they left the house.

The Spinners decided that the safest place to be was the St. George's Police Station. They decided to go down to the station and just hang around outside until Inspector Savage showed up. By sticking so close to the station, Tattoo Jack wouldn't dare try anything. Instead of going the direct route to the station they chose to avoid Queen Street and loop around the back of town via the Unfinished Cathedral. Believing they were probably being watched, the Spinners climbed the stone wall on the side of the house, avoiding the obvious front gate. The storm had really kicked in now. There was now heavy winds and rain, mixed with thunder and lightening. It was only mid-afternoon, but it was abnormally very dark. The kids are running down the street trying to get out of sight of Graham's house. As they ran down the street, Gunner spotted them just as they disappeared across the street. He immediately called out on the walkie talkie.

"They're heading over to Kent Street, and there are five of them."

Tattoo chimed in: "Everyone converges on Kent Street. Now!"

As the Spinners got within sight of the Unfinished Cathedral they saw Tattoo's truck coming up the hill from the opposite direction. Now they knew they were going to be trapped. Panic set in.

Keno said as he pulled out the cross from his pocket. "This is want there after. Let's just leave it here on the street for them."

"Hell no!" Michael said. "Once they get the cross they'll get rid of us. Keno, throw me the cross." Keno did. Portagee glanced down at his compass momentarily. It was hooked on his belt loop and the needle was spinning like crazy. He ignored the phenomenon and went on listening.

Graham said, "Look, our only chance is to cut through the archway on the west side of the Cathedral. Then we'll sneak out the back and lose them."

Everybody agreed and they ran like banshees to the Cathedral.

Tattoo's goons were now hot on their heels. As the Spinners neared the archway they noticed a remarkable feature. Smack on the upper half of the arch was a perfect tri-

angle made out of raised stone. Michael was the first to reach the archway entrance. He was holding the cross in his right hand and as he stepped towards the entrance the triangle portion of the archway began emanating electromagnetic waves. The emeralds in the cross appeared to respond to this phenomenon and fired a triangular green laser beam into the centre of the stone triangle. Simultaneously, lightening bolts were striking the electromagnetic waves. As each of the Spinners passed through the gateway a bright green electronic blast occurred. Just as the last Spinner, Graham, was about to enter the gateway he was tackled by Gunner and Cuda. A blast occurred and they all hit the side of the archway and fell to the ground unconscious. There were a few more rapid mini green explosions in the gateway and then it abruptly ended, just as it had started. Tattoo, Sledge and Axle reached the Unfinished Cathedral soon after, only to find Graham, Gunner and Cuda lying silent on the ground.

Tattoo yelled, "Sledge, get in there and find those kids."

Sledge charged through the archway, thoroughly scanning the Cathedral but found no sign of them. Tattoo reached down and started shaking Gunner and Cuda to bring them back around. The two slowly got up. All of them just stood there, staring at Graham.

Axle said, "He looks dead."

Graham just lay there motionless with blood running down his face.

Tattoo said, "I can't tell whether he's dead or not. Let's scram before somebody sees us. This snot-nosed kid's father is Thomas Aston the Chairman of Aston Petroleum. He's also personal friends with the Governor and the Premier. Axle, no one will miss you. You keep looking for the other brats. Gunner and Sledge get down to the "Black Shark", Cuda, you come with me in the truck and we'll head to the Shinbone. If anyone asks, we've been between the boat and the Shinbone all day. Now move it!"

Twenty minutes later Graham started to gain consciousness... He felt dazed and confused. For a moment he couldn't remember where he was. Finally he struggled to his feet, looked around, and yelled, "Spinners, where the heck are you?"

No answer.

He walked around the Cathedral and saw no trace of anyone. Graham then remembered that a couple of weeks ago Portagee rigged all of their GPS cell phones with a "Spinners" find button. Once the button was pushed it would list each Spinner. Then if you "clicked" on their name it would tell you within a hundred yards where that particular Spinner physically was. He flipped open the phone, tapped the "Spinners" button, but nothing happened. Nobody showed up on the phone. What were the odds that all four of them had their phones off? He sat down and began recalling the events that led up to where he was now.

Looking at the archway and seeing a few scorch marks on the stone it came back to him. This was a gateway to the Bermuda Triangle and the Tucker Cross must have been the key to the gateway. Yes, that must be the answer, thought Graham. Then he sat down on one of the stone walls and said out loud, "Holy Smoke! Who in the world is going to believe this"!

He decided he better go down to the St. George's Police department and wait for Sam's father, Inspector Savage.

About 7:15pm Inspector Savaged arrived at the Station and Graham was waiting for him just outside the doorway.

Savage saw Graham, stopped, threw his arm around him and said, "Graham, what are you doing here tonight?"

Almost in tears, Graham said, "Waiting for you sir."

Graham went on and told Inspector Savage what had happened. By now, they were both sitting down on the curb and Savage was blown away by Graham's story.

Finally Savage said, "Graham, are you sure you're OK? That's a nasty bump on your bean."

"Yes sir,", Graham replied.

Savage then went on to say, "Graham, I'm going to set your story aside for now. First, I've got to call your parents and have them come get you and take you to the emergency room to get your head checked. Then I'm going to call all the other parents and see if any of your friends are home yet. Maybe they're just playing a joke on you, but maybe they're all scared to death and are just hiding from Mr. Skinner. After that, I plan on paying Mr. Skinner a visit."

It took a couple of hours to get Graham off to the hospital and all the parents and grandparents called. By 9:30 p.m. nobody had heard from any of the missing kids. At this point even Inspector Savage losing hope, but he couldn't even file a Missing Person's Report yet on any of them until twenty four hours passed. The whole thing was just so eerie: a missing group of kids that call themselves "Spinners" for Tall Tales. Even though his hands were tied the Inspector was still going down to the Shinbone Pub to pay Mr. Skinner a visit.

Savage entered the Shinbone and as expected there sat Tattoo and his thugs.

"Evening Inspector. What brings you down to mix with the common folk tonight?" Tattoo said.

Savage responded, "Don't flatter yourself Skinner. I've got four missing kids tonight and another beaten up in the hospital right now as I speak. Can you shed some light on any of this Mr. Skinner?"

Tattoo responded, "Well Inspector, me and my mates have been here most of the day planning our next month's fishing trips. We haven't a clue about your missing kids."

Savage reckoned that this was going to be hard going as Skinner was very sly.

"Skinner!" barked Savage, "One of these kids says your thugs were tailing them today. Is that right?"

"No Sir", responded Tattoo.

"Well Skinner", replied Savage, "I'll be putting an officer on guard aboard the "Black Shark", so make sure you don't plan any fishing trips for the next few days. And, furthermore, I expect you to leave your passport at the Police Station by noon tomorrow. Do you understand Skinner?"

"I understand. You'll be hearing from my attorney tomorrow. You can't harass innocent people like this!" countered Tattoo.

Savage turned about face, left the pub and headed back up the street to the Police Station. He said a little prayer for the safe return of his daughter and her friends.

10

PARADISE IN THE TRIANGLE

I n a flash and a bang the Spinners were thrown on to a beach. They all lay motion-less as the ocean waves rolled over their limp bodies.

They were now in the Bermuda Triangle.

Because no one has ever returned from the "Devil's" or "Bermuda" Triangle it has never been factually described before. It is actually another dimension in time. Some might describe it as a "Twilight Zone", or even "Never Land". The apexes of the triangle are Bermuda, Miami, Fla., and San Juan, Puerto Rico. Whatever gateway you enter the triangle you will find yourself being close to parallel to the same space you left before you went into the Triangle. So in fact if you entered the Triangle in the Atlantic Ocean you would still find yourself in the Atlantic Ocean, except in a different dimen-sion. It might take you days or weeks to realize you had been transported. The only clues you would have, is that compasses would just spin around in circles and guidance and communication equipment would no longer function. You would be confined to the defined area of the Triangle and would just find yourself going around in circles. If you entered the Triangle on a land mass, such as Bermuda, you would still be in Bermuda except you might think you were in a distant paradise. The island is in the pristine state as it was over 500 years ago before anyone ever stepped foot on the tiny island. The wild hogs are still ruminating on the island and if you bothered to notice there are other extinct animals, birds, plants and fish to be found.

The only hope of returning to the dimension, from which you came, is to find a gateway back, but there is no record of this ever having happened. The balance of nature in the Triangle is simple. The existing life in the Triangle evolves and reproduces just like our parallel world; however, if you are a species from another dimension, you enter it sterile. Thus, you can exist in the Triangle but you cannot populate it. Yes, by the way, it is a Never Land in which you will remain the same age as you entered. You can die there; you can be injured or killed just like anyone in our dimension. You just won't age or get any disease of our world. While time stands still in the Triangle, it marches on in our dimension. So if anyone was to ever find a way to return from the Triangle you would not re-enter in your time in history, but at the time that had lapsed while you were gone. There are few humans alive in the Triangle today. Most people enter the Triangle from airplanes and ships entering temporary gateways in the middle of the Triangle, which is the Atlantic Ocean. Most planes run out of fuel before finding any land mass, crash in the ocean and unfortunately the occupants drown. Most ships usually enter the Triangle through a raging storm or hurricane and are severely damaged on their arrival. They might sink soon after their arrival or even worst, because they cannot find any land mass without any sense of direction, the sailors and passengers may simply starve to death or die of thirst. This leaves many ghost ships floating around the waters of the Triangle.

The Triangle is truly a paradise when left alone, however, at times when evil outsiders enter the dimension, the paradisiacal balance is spoiled. As in our world, Mother Nature is normally able to maintain a reasonably natural balance. Except at the present time, for the past three hundred years an overwhelming invasion of evil beings have entered the Triangle. Mother Nature needs lots of help.

Can the "Spinners" fill this roll?

11

LIFE IN THE TRIANGLE

During World War II the Germans sent several submarines to monitor the east coast of the United States. The German submarine "Wolf Blitz" was a special Nazi SS spy sub commanded by Nazi SS officer Stryker von Hammer. Stryker is a ruthless cold-blooded killer who lost his left eye from a shrapnel explosion during the invasion of France. Stryker was amazingly comfortable in a spy sub. After all, you only need one eye to look out of a periscope. Stryker's submarine was on a spy mission to the United States and was lost in the Devil's Triangle in 1944. The sub spent weeks in the triangle trying to determine its location, but the sub's batteries were draining and there was precious little fuel and food left. Then, all of a sudden, the sub crossed paths with Bermuda. The sub made shore on the West end of the island, where the Dockyard would be today. Eventually the sub was washed ashore during a hurricane. Today it serves as an impregnable mini fortress for the Nazis if they were attacked. Any local invaders would have no weapons to breach the solid steel hull of the sealed sub.

Captain Drax and his pirates did survive the explosion in the cave. They were drawn into the Triangle when a vacuum formed with the collapse of the cave. Although totally confused, with no concept of where they were, they ended up settling. They created a small fortress at the east end of the island, in the approximate geographic area of St. George's.

There were also a small group of Confederate blockade runners during the American Civil War that would sneak through the Union coastal blockade to sail to Bermuda and trade cotton for food and weapons. One of these small blockade runner ships was caught up in a severe electromagnetic storm southwest of Bermuda in 1862 when they entered the Bermuda Triangle. Although most of the crew survived the storm, they made the unfortunate decision to land at the east end of the island. Drax and his cutthroats were ready for them and massacred most of the Confederate sailors. A few of them escaped and found refuge in the centre of the island.

In 1953, a British pilot on a top secret trip from Jamaica to Bermuda was lost in the Triangle but was lucky enough to find Bermuda and then even luckier when he stumbled upon the group of Confederates in the centre of the island.

A US Navy bomber on a patrol mission out of the US in 1956 was not as fortunate as the British pilot. This plane crashed at sea after entering the Triangle. Two of the crew managed to use their rubber raft and floated with the Gulf Stream currents to Bermuda. They were captured by the Nazis who still thought the war was still raging. They were tortured for weeks for war information, by Commander Stryker. One escaped his captors and found refuge in the middle of the island, but the other Yank was tortured to death.

There are others who survived the Triangle and lucked out by finding the middle of the island before the pirates or the Nazis found them.

Present day life in the Triangle or at least at the Bermuda end of the Triangle is very challenging. At each end of the island you have cutthroats and killers that will do anything to survive. Because each group is small in size and gradually shrinking, they can only barely hold and protect their small portion of the tiny island. They make weekly excursions deep into the central part of the island for supplies and conquest. In the early days of these encounters, the Nazis had the upper hand. Their weapons were superior to those of the pirates, but having been on a small submarine their weapons were also very limited. They soon ran out of ammunition, and with no way to replenish it they had to resort to using muskets and sabers that they found on the island washed up from the old ghost ships. Neither of the warring factions really understood where they were. The pirates were still hunting for treasure while the Nazis still thought they were at war. Both Drax and Stryker are indiscriminate killers and will stop at nothing to achieve their goals. The mixture of people in the middle of the island just try to survive and stay clear of the warring factions. Many of the more recent Triangle survivors somehow understood where they were and were always seeking ways to escape the Triangle.

As the waves rolled over the Spinners, one by one they began to wake up. They helped each other get to their feet and shuffled off the beach.

Keno spoke up first, "I remember going through the archway at the Cathedral, and then I saw a flash, that's it!"

Michael looked around and said, "Where's Graham?"

Nobody knew.

Sam said, "Are we on the North Shore? I don't recognize this beach?"

As they sat there, they all gawked and stared out at the ocean hoping to get their bearings. If they were on the North Shore all they should see would be the ocean, no land. Instead, just about a mile away they discerned some land.

Portagee said, "You know what? That looks like Hamilton Harbour over there, except where are the houses and office buildings?"

When he pulled out his compass, it was spinning.

"Look at this"; Portagee said as he showed everyone his compass. "This is exactly what the compass was doing when I got close to the archway at the Cathedral."

Keno looked at Michael and said, "Are you thinking what I'm thinking?"

Michael responded, "Yes, I reckon we've stumbled inside the Bermuda Triangle."

Sam said, "You're nuts, let me try to call home", she flipped open her phone and nothing the battery was dead. "That's strange I just charged the battery last night", she said. The others then all checked their cell phones, same results, all the batteries were dead. "OK then, it looks like were in what to us would be the Dockyard. So we entered the Triangle in St. George's and came out at the other end of the island at the Dockyard", Michael said. Keno responded, "Then that means we have to get back to St. George's to the gateway we entered through", "That's right", Portagee said, 'Except what if the Cathedral archway isn't there, then what. Wait I know, Shark Hole has the similar level of electromagnetic waves and it should be there naturally". Keno then chimed in, "Look out there in the harbor, there's some old wooden ship wrecks". Everyone looked; they were amazed at the site. Sam was thinking, and then said, "Bermuda is many islands connected by bridges, and I'm thinking that there are no bridges here, were going to have to swim or float a lot". They all agreed she was right. It was getting late the Spinners agreed that they better first find a shelter for the night. They climbed up over one of the small dunes behind them, and then undergrowth was thick and hard to move through. As they came to what they thought was a small clearing Michael pushed aside the tall grass and froze. The rest of the Spinners also stop dead in their tracks when they saw what Michael saw. The group had accidentally stumbled onto the back side of the Nazi encampment. There were small huts surrounding a grounded German submarine, the most visible and bone chilling view was the large Nazi flag flying over the sub with a smaller SS flag waving just below it, the large Swastika was frightening. All of the kids had enough history lessons to understand that these people were ruthless killers of the Third Reich and not to be messed with. They all slowly backed away letting the tall grass go and went back to their more remote beach. On the way back they found some bananas trees so as least tonight they would have something to eat. The Dockyard is located on a fairly long but narrow island that was called Ireland Island North. The Spinners were truly cut off from the rest of Bermuda with the Nazis blocking their way. The Nazi were encamped on the harbor side of the small island, in the morning the Spinners could take their chances of sneaking around them on the opposite side of the island, along the outer beach.

The next morning back in Bermuda, Inspector Savage went to the St. George's police station very early, although he could still not send out an APB on the children he could still do other things. First he called the Harbor Patrol to have them keep an eye out for the children on several of the tiny islands in the Bermuda harbors that people like to go camping on. He was still thinking that maybe they just went out camping for a couple of days and just failed to take Graham along as some type of joke. He then decided to go up to the Unfinished Cathedral; if Graham's story had any validity he might find some clues. When he got to the Cathedral he went to the west side to check the archway, as Graham had stated there were some scorched markings around the archway. They were fairly new and still carried a burnt scent on them. Inspector Savage then began to take note of the footprints in and out of the archway. Since it rained heavy yesterday, the footprints were very clear and legible. It was obvious that there were four to six sets of very defined sets of prints on the outside of the archway, however on the inside of the archway it was just as muddy but there was only one to two sets of prints. The Inspector thought to himself four to six in and one to two out, where did they go, they didn't back out of the archway. He kept thinking about Graham's story about the gateway to the Bermuda Triangle, "No that's impossible ", he thought. Inspector Savage then spoke into his police radio, "This is Savage calling base, please come in", "Roger", replied the dispatcher, "Send up a forensics officer to take casts of some footprints, some pictures and take some samples of some burnt markings", replied Savage. The dispatcher replied, "Roger an officer is on his way now", "Thanks", replied Salvage, "I'll wait for him to arrive, over and out".

12

NAZI WAR MONGERS

The Spinners were up before daybreak and made their way to the Nazi encampment. Through the tall grass they watched the camp break for the morning. It appeared that there were about eleven of them, a full WWII crew would have been about twenty five.

The Commander with a patch over his left eye barked out some commands in German and three of the crew picked up their muskets and left camp, looks like they were going hunting, but what were they hunting. They left in the direction that the Spinners would be going also. Three more of the crew went towards the harbor carrying some buckets. The other four appeared to just mill around the camp. While the commander pulled out his saber and began hacking at a cedar tree stump. Maybe he was practicing his swordsmanship. The Spinners agreed that this was one person to stay away from.

The Spinners knew they had to get off Ireland Island North quickly, this island was very narrow and there chances to being seen were too great. If they could get on to Somerset Island, then on to the main island they could get lost in the forest and hills. Michael signaled the group to back up out of the tall grass and began to move towards the ocean side beach. They found a swinging rope bridge connecting the two Ireland

Islands. One at a time inched across the bridge making sure the Nazi patrol did not happen upon them. Staying on the north shoreline of the island appeared to be the safest route, the hog trails all stayed to the central part of the island; this is where they thought the Nazis would be traveling. All went fairly well and quickly, when they were ready to enter the ocean to swim to the next island they realized that there were two smaller islands in front of them to go through before getting to Somerset Island, Boaz and Watford Island's. No problem just more too clear, back in the other world with roads and bridges sometimes it was hard to tell when you went from one island to another. Just to make sure they were not being watched they swam one at a time with a distance between them of about fifty yards. Boaz Island was small with no beaches, only jagged rocks on the shore. They were forced to move into the dense jungle area. Halfway through the island Keno signaled everyone to hit the ground. He thought he had heard something. No other sounds were heard so they started through the brush again. They came across a narrow path, probably a goat or hog trail and decided to follow it. Portagee was third in line, just following the other and not paying attention, he took another step and "swish"; he was jerked up in the air by his right foot and was bouncing up and down hanging upside down. Portagee had been caught in some type of animal trap. Portagee was screaming, while the others were trying to calm him down. Keno pulled out his pocket knife and began cutting on the rope while Michael and Sam tried to hold Portagee up and take some of the pressure off the rope. Finally Keno cut through the rope, Michael and Sam slowly lowered Portagee to the ground. When everyone calmed down Sam said, "We better get moving, I'm sure whatever that sound we thought we heard awhile ago has now heard us". She was right the Nazi patrol had heard the commotion in the area from their traps and were heading that direction. The Spinners quickly moved on, they found a small man made plank bridge to Watford Island, this island was so small they cleared it in about 10 minutes. They had to take another dip in the ocean to get to Somerset Island. This island was much larger and it took a good while to cross it, the Spinners felt they were well ahead of the Nazis, that is, if they were being followed, so they stayed on the trail that appeared to cut through the island. After reaching the end of Somerset Island they had just one more small swim to make it to the main island. This island was much wider and the Spinners took advantage of that and moved off the trail and headed for higher ground.

The Nazi patrol arrived at the trap about fifteen minutes after the Spinners had left. They saw the trap had been sprung and that the rope had been cut, they knew now that they had caught a person not an animal. Two of the patrol went on down the trail to try to find the person, while the third member looked around the area for clues. After a couple of minutes he saw a black object under a bush. It was Portagee's billfold; it must have fallen out of his pocket when he was hanging upside down. By now the other patrol members had returned to see what he had. They opened up the billfold and saw a student ID with a picture of Portagee, across from it was a picture of all the Spinners. He them said, "Look it's a boy and maybe his friends, we better get this back to Stryker quickly". The three came running into the camp, the crew member with the billfold was yelling, "Stryker, Stryker, Stryker". Stryker looked up and went over to men and said, "What is it, what are you excited about"? The crew member handed him the billfold and told him the story about the trap. Stryker looked thru the billfold with pain staking patience, he found the student ID, Bermuda two dollar bill, a US one dollar bill and the picture of the Spinners. Our enemies are sending children to spy on us. We must hunt them down find out what they are doing here and then kill them, I don't care if they are children, they are still the enemies of the Third Reich", Stryker said loudly, then he clicked his boot heels together and yelled, "Search the area and see if they were here spying on us". The Nazis moved out in all directions looking for clues. The Nazis found the beach area where they had spent the night and consumed the bananas. They also found the area in the tall grass where they had been watched. Stryker felt that someone or some force had landed the spy's on the beach and then left them there to spy and maybe to pick them up later. He now felt that the Allies may have finally found this lost island and was out to destroy them; this meant the war must still be going on. Stryker addressed his troops, "Tonight prepare your kits, clean your weapons, for tomorrow will track down those English and American dogs. Five of you will go with me and five will stay and guard the encampment".

The Spinners kept moving as quickly as possible. They knew which way they needed to go but because the roads and landmarks that they were used to were not there it was very difficult. In the late afternoon they swam across a narrow channel Somerset Island to Bermuda Island itself. They were tired and hungry and scared. Finally they found a small grouping of bananas trees in what appeared to be a safe out of the way area. Keno and Michael had found a few fallen coconuts back on the shoreline in hopes to drink the milk later. When they sat and ate and drank the coconut milk they reevaluated their positions and plans. Sam was the first to recap her thoughts, "OK, were probably being followed right now by some gun happy Nazis. We're on our way to Shark Hole in hopes to find our way out of the Triangle. Do we think that the Nazis are the only ones here beside ourselves? If they were why would they be held up at the Dockyard, something must be keeping them there. Also with all these ships and ship wrecks we saw around Hamilton harbor there must be some survivors from those ships. Everyone agreed with Sam, believing that there were many more surprises that lay in front of them and they needed to be extremely cautious. Michael then pulled out the "Tucker Cross" from his pocket and held it up. He then said," Let's not forget this cross; it's the key to the Triangle. We must protect it and make sure no one takes this from us. Maybe at some point in time we may need to hide the cross. Remember Tattoo wanted it for its value and it may be the same here". "Your right", replied Keno. It was time now to get some sleep, they all said good night to each other and tried to sleep as well as they could without blankets or a fire.

The 24 hour time requirement had now passed and Inspector Savage has filed the Missing Persons Reports for Sam, Michael, and Keno and Portagee. Savage had also met with all the families to assure them that everything was being done to find the kids. Thomas Aston had also posted a $10,000.00 reward for information leading for the location of the children. Tattoo Jack and all his thugs had been interrogated one by one by the police department. Except for some footprints they had nothing to pin on Tattoo Jack and his men. They were released and free to move around the island, however they did have to surrender their passports. Inspector Savage made sure Tattoo and all his men were under constant surveillance. Tattoo knew they were all being watched and acted according. Tattoo was still obsessed with finding the "Tucker Cross". He had twice in the last 72 hours had the "Tucker Cross" within his grasp, only to elude him once again. He and his men were as confused as Inspector Savage and the police department were. He had been at the Unfinished Cathedral at the time of the explosions and the Spinners mysteriously vanishing without explanation. Tattoo was keeping close tabs on Graham; he still thought he knew where the Spinners were hiding.

13

PILGRIMS TO THE RESCUE

On the surface, it appeared to be simply another beautiful sunrise in paradise, but the Spinners had failed to appreciate that. They were all too nervous. The island, void of all memorable landmarks, made it almost impossible for them to know where they were. Without being able to see the South shoreline or having a visual sighting of Hamilton Harbour, they intuitively believed that they were going in the right direction, but that was about all. The plan for Today's goal was to head generally towards Hamilton Harbour, get their bearings and then proceed to Shark Hole. The hiking was slow since they had to deal with the dense undergrowth. The sun was already almost directly overhead, so they knew it was nearing noon. Keno was leading the group. He was the strongest and probably knew Bermuda best. Suddenly, Keno raised his hand and stopped.

He exclaimed, "Look... a hog trail, it looks like it heads to the harbour. Let's follow it." They were all so tired of dealing with the thick undergrowth that they agreed to follow the trail, forgetting the fact that this might be dangerous and leave them more exposed. It was definitely much easier going and they started to make very good time. As they came up to a small clearing, Keno signaled it was time to take a break. Tired, they all sat down.

Portagee then said, "I wonder if the Nazis are still looking for us?"

Then all of a sudden the Spinners heard clicking sounds all around them from within the tall growth.

A voice with a foreign accent then spoke, "Now we have found you, you spies."

Then Stryker and his SS men stepped out into the open.

"Don't make any sudden moves if you value your lives", Stryker told them. He then continued, "You are prisoners of war. Who is your leader?"

As he looked around, Michael stepped forward and said, "That would be me."

Stryker smiled and said, "You're an American."

Michael nodded.

"I despise Americans." Stryker yelled back, "You're a bunch of inferior inbreeds. How about the rest of you?"

They all said "Bermudians" at the same time.

Stryker responded, "Then you are English, but your accents sound different." He then turned back to Michael and said, "Well Mr. Leader, why are you spying on us and who dropped you off on the beach?"

Michael replied, "We're not spies. We're simply lost."

"You lie," barked Stryker as he hit Michael with the back of his hand, knocking him to the ground. Stryker started kicking Michael repeatedly with his steel capped boots. The SS men had to restrain the others as they tried to go to Michael's rescue.

Michael looked up and said, "You Nazi creep."

The furious Stryker stared at Michael and drew out his saber. Making a round-house swing with the saber he screamed, "You American dog, meet your maker!"

As the saber was swinging down at Michael three shots rang out. The saber snapped off at the handle. One of the SS men was hit in the temple by a bullet and collapsed; another SS man was hit in the chest. He also collapsed. The Nazi was dead before he hit the ground. In the confusion several bodies streaked through the clearing grabbing the Spinners by the arms and then running down the twisting path and out of sight. Stryker was now on the ground, not knowing for sure what had just happened. Two of his men futility fired their muskets down the path at the runners, but it was too late. They were already out of sight.

Stryker, then kicked the other SS man who was lying down on the ground covering his head, and said, "Get up you coward." He then assessed the situation and realized that two of his men were dead. Stryker kicked the ground. He was beside himself. He had just lost two men he couldn't afford to lose and he had just lost his young prisoners as well.

He then turned to his men and said, "Pick them up and let's head back to camp." He had suffered a big enough defeat for one day.

The Spinners were running for their lives along with their liberators, whoever they were. After running about half a kilometer they reached a ridge and their liberators stopped to rest. One man in a uniform turned and asked if they were all O.K... They all nodded yes.

He then said, "Let us introduce ourselves. I'm an RAF pilot and my name is Jason. We go by first names only. Just behind you is a US pilot, Spence and to your right are two Confederate blockade runners, Buford and Bubba. When we get to the boat, I'll brief you more fully. Oh, by the way, you do know that you're in the Bermuda Triangle?"

Michael said, "Yes."

Then the kids introduced themselves.

Jason then said, "Let's get going, I think Stryker has given up, but let's not take any more chances." So off they went. Soon they cleared a small hill and to the Spinners' amazement they were overlooking Hamilton Harbour. It was beautiful...... totally unspoiled by man. There were no towering buildings and not a single house, only a clear aquamarine harbour, gorgeous plant life, and magnificent cedars surrounding the harbour.

Spence said, "Home is over there." He pointed towards what we know as Hamilton.

Now the group hiked down toward the water. They arrived at a tiny semi-hidden cove where they had a longboat covered with brush. The liberators pulled the boat out from under the brush and slipped it into the water.

"Everyone scramble in," Spence said.

It was incredible. They were all getting into a longboat that was probably over 300 years old. There were patches all over it where they had done whatever it took to keep it seaworthy. Buford and Bubba took the oars and began rowing while the rest of the group chatted excitedly and looked around in amazement.

"We have found it safer to live in the central part of the island," Jason said, "Incidentally; our Nazi friends are not our only problem. At the east end of the island in what you would have known as St. George's is a band of cutthroat pirates led by Captain Drax. They are a drunken bunch, totally unpredictable and would just a soon kill you as look at you. At least with the Nazis, who by the way still think there's a war on, you can at least expect a military strategy. You have already seen their ruthless killers. Then there are the rest of us. We're a small group of survivors from different times and places who were lucky enough not to be killed by the Nazis or the pirates on our arrival."

As they rowed by Hinson's Island Jason said, "That Island is where we have stored some emergency rations and goods in case we ever have to flee our settlement. Oh, we don't keep track of time here. We figure why bother....I mean what year is it anyway?"

Sam responded, "It's the year 2005."

Spence said, "Holly crap, I'm an old man now, I'm over 80."

Bubba laughed and said, "Yeh and I'm a dead man now, I'm.......I'm."

Buford chimed in, "You dumb ass, you can't count that high, your over 150 years old."

The mouths of all the Spinners just dropped open.

"Our settlement is out at what you kids would have known as the Spanish Point area," Jason said. "There we have a good vantage point. We can keep an eye on what enters the harbour and still keep an eye on the Nazis. In fact that is how we knew you were here. We saw you camped on the beach with our telescope. We were on our way to rescue you because we realized that Stryker would think you were some type of spies. I'm impressed with you kids though.... you managed to sneak through his lines without getting caught."

Keno laughed and then said, "Sure, but he still caught us with our pants down."

Michael added, "And if it weren't for you gentlemen, I would be dead by now."

Spence said, "Don't worry. That's what were here for, to protect the tourists."

Then everyone laughed. Spence pointed out some of the old wrecks.

"These wrecks are where we find supplies, food, weapons, ammunition, rum and whatever else we think we may need. Needless to say we can't produce anything here and there are no importers either," he then smiled, "We have to keep an eye out for new wrecks or small lost sailboats to float in. Then it's a fight to see who gets there first."

They were now getting closer to shore. Buford looked up and saw Keno staring at his gray uniform; Buford thought it might be a good time to address it.

"Keno, just in case this might be an issue for you, Bubba and I were just poor swamp farmers and gator trappers back in Louisiana when the war broke out. We did-n't have any Negro slaves, in fact we didn't believe in slavery. We went to war because those damn Yankees invaded our land. Just thought you might want to know, that in our minds and God's, all men are created equal."

Keno blithely lied: "No, that never entered my mind." But it really had, but now he was a little more relieved. Spence added, "Since I'm from Wisconsin they call me a Yankee. I had to break it to them that the South got their butts kicked and lost the war."

Then they all laughed. They now maneuvered the longboat around a tiny over-grown island, the Spinners knew this island as Saltus Island and just behind it was what appeared to be the shoreline with heavy bushes growing all over it. The boat made contact with the bushes and did not hit ground; these were hanging bushes that had fully concealed a small cove known as Soncy Cove in the other world. As the longboat cleared the bushes the Spinners saw a small sandy beach with two other longboats tied to large cedar trees. Everyone got out of the boat, pulled it up on shore and tied it to another cedar tree.

Sam said, "This is an ideal private beach for swimming."

Spence said, "Your right, except remember the waters here have never been fished commercially. The water is teaming with fish and because of that they're also teaming with predators: sharks and barracudas. So you do need to be very careful even this close to land."

Jason looked at the sun said, "It's getting late. We'd better get moving before it gets any darker."

About fifty yards up from the beach they came across a trail that would get them back to Spanish Point. About a half hour later it was really getting dark. They were close to the settlement entrance and the Spinners recognized the area that they used to know as Admiralty House Park. Jason raised his hand to signal the group to stop.

After a few seconds they heard someone say from behind the gate, "Stop, who's here?"

Bubba laughed and said, "Cooter, your supposed to say, stop who's there?"

Cooter a little confused sputtered, "Dangnadit Bubba, you know what I mean."

They all laughed and waited for Cooter to open the gate. As they walked by Bubba said, "Everyone, this is cousin Cooter."

Cooter replied, "Hi y'all, glad to meet ya'."

Cooter then closed the gate after everyone was in. The group went to the centre of the camp where a large fire was burning.

Spence said, "Is dinner ready?"

Lynn said, "Well of course. The boys caught rock fish today and we have sweet Bermuda onions and avocados, I see you found the lost ones."

"Your right Lynn," said Jason, "Let me introduce our little family. Lynn and Tom arrived thirty years ago on a sailing boat. Johnny, an African American was washed ashore from a ship wreck sixty-six years ago. He was the ship's doctor and has been an invaluable asset to the settlement. The family now just calls him Doc. Next there is,

Georgette. Her single engine plane crashed just off the coast on a trans-continental flight from France to the U.S. fifty-seven years ago. You already met Cooter, Bubba's cousin, and last but not least is Salty, he arrived here with Captain Drax. He was the ship's cook with a peg leg. He tells everyone a shark bit his leg off when he was a young man. Salty is the oldest man on the island, must be about two hundred seventy five years young and he doesn't look over fifty."

Michael asked, "Salty, if you were with the pirates, how did you get here?"

Salty replied, "Well whipper-snapper, after cook in' for Drax and the cutthroats for 100 years I got sick of it and up and left. I eventually found my friends the Johnny Rebs and here I am. Let's all eat, I'm hungry".

While they were eating the Spinners introduced themselves to the group. After dinner Jason took the kids to one of the spare huts where they could sleep. He then had Sam move into the hut with Georgette. The old ship's clock showed it was 10pm, everyone had already turned in for the night, except for Tom and Doc, they had the night watch detail. Tom would be on watch until 2am and then Doc would take the 2am to daylight shift. It was a full moon so watching the camp would be much easier tonight. All was calm tonight after such a violent day.

Daily life in the Spanish Point area settlement was very basic, each person had their own daily chores to perform for the settlement and when they finished they could do whatever they wanted to. This morning the Spinners tagged along with whoever they felt comfortable. After lunch the group sat down to discuss the events of the week. Everyone was worried that the Nazis would want to take out revenge killings on the settlement; however, the attack to save the Spinners happened so quickly that the Nazis may not even be sure who attacked them.

Sam was not clear from last night's conversations why there were only three survivors from the blockade runner's ship. Buford then begin to retell the story.

"In 1862 west of Bermuda their ship ran head on into a major hurricane. The ship survived, they sailed on for days. As they tried to land in what they thought was Bermuda their damaged ship struck a reef off shore. This was this crew's first trip to Bermuda and none of them knew what the island looked like. The ship began sinking and the captain commanded the crew to abandon ship. As the crew swam for shore it appeared that a patrol of British solders were waiting for them. Their uniforms were strange and different, but we had never seen a British solider before either. The three of us were last off the ship. Cooter couldn't swim so we had to find him an empty barrel to hang on to while me and Bubba held on to each side and headed for shore. By the time we were in the water most of the crew was walking onto the beach. Our captain went directly toward the British captain, saluted him and then extended his hand out to shake his. At that same moment the British captain drew his saber and ran it threw our captain. That's when all hell broke loose. The rest of the patrol began shooting and slic-

ing up our fellow crew members with their hog stickers. They were massacred in minutes. We then started swimming further down the coast, the killers never saw us out in the ocean. As we later spied on their camp, we then realized that they were pirates and we were probably not in Bermuda. A few years later we were lucky enough to run into Salty. And that's it, Cooter still can't swim and he still can't chase down a hog or a goat."

Everyone then laughed.

Keno then said, "Where do the wild goats come from? There were wild hogs but no goats in the other Bermuda."

Spence smiled and said, "Over the years we've had them swim ashore from ship wrecks. Since they're sterile we only ate the males and kept the females for milking.

"Now that's enough about us," Jason added. "Tell us more about you. You seem to think that if you get to this Shark Hole you can get back to the world we all left."

Michael stood up and responded, "We entered a gateway to the Triangle during a very heavy lightening storm. We used a key to open the gateway so we could enter. Unfortunately we didn't know any of this at the time."

"So there's a key to the Triangle, then where is it?"

Michael turned to Sam and said, "Please hand me the cross, Sam."

She opened up her backpack reached and pulled out the Tucker Cross.

Salty choked on his drink and spit it out then jumped up and started screaming,

"That's it, that's it, that's the cross that Captain Drax had in the cave the night of the collapse. It shot out bright green lightening bolts. I will never forget what I saw that night."

The Spinners were surprised, but Salty confirmed their theory. Michael passed the cross around the table for the others to look at it.

Michael then said, "Portagee discovered that the Shark Hole appears to have the same electromagnetic waves emitting from it, as did the gateway we entered. We need to go there and see if we can open the gateway to return to the other side."

Salty then said, "You need to be very careful. Captain Drax believes in the occult and witchcraft. He thinks that that cross has magical powers. If he knows it's here he will stop at nothing to get it."

Michael said, "Shark Hole is not close to St. George's, he need never know."

"Don't be so sure. He has his men out on patrol everywhere," Spence chimed in. "Alright then," Spence said. "Besides the kids and myself, let's take Bubba and Cooter. Jason let me see your map."

Jason has an old pilot's map with Bermuda on it. The map's okay, just not very detailed. "To save time we'll set a longboat in the water here and row along North Shore and set ashore just this side of Flatts inlet."

Bubba said, "Why don't we just row into the inlet and on into Harrington Sound. That would save at least an hour."

"You're right," said Spence, "Except our presence would be seen from all over the Sound." "Hadn't thought of that", muttered Bubba. "We'd be better off hiking in from North Shore, quickly test your theory and get out of there."

Cooter issued sabers to Portagee, Keno, Sam and Michael. Then he demonstrated how to defend himself with just a saber.

"We'll leave in an hour," Spence said.

Then he and Bubba went down to the shore to get the longboat ready.

14

FINDING SHARK HOLE

The longboat shoved off with their crew aboard and, as expected, Bubba and Cooter were manning the oars. Cooter said, "At first I was excited to go on this trip, now I know why you really wanted us." Spence smiled and said, "No, that's not true, keep rowing."

The waters today around the island were as smooth as glass and bright turquoise in color. It was easy to see how one could easily be lost in the serene beauty of these surroundings.

Portagee was at the front of the boat swinging his saber out over the water and saying, "Yo Ho Ho, Matey."

Finally Michael told him to sit down and enjoy the ride. With the calm water and no wind they made much better time than expected. Just before the Flatts inlet is a small cove which they rowed into, with very little chance of being seen. Bubba and Cooter pulled the longboat up off the beach and covered it with some palm leaves.

Spence said, "Make sure your muskets are primed and ready.... just in case. Bubba fall in behind me and Cooter you bring up the rear."

Cooter said, "I know, they always pick off the last guy."

"Shut up." Spence said, "Keep in single file. We'll try to move along the shoreline of the Sound just above the tree line so no one will be able to spot us. If anything goes wrong and we get separated, just head back here and wait for the others."

At this point the Spinners were getting very jittery, but they knew they were close to Shark Hole and stood a good chance to return home. The hiking was hard along the uneven rocky shore line. Shark Hole was in the south east corner of Harrington Sound. It was evident that the entrance was covered with vines hanging down to the water. The cave was usually half submerged in water since the sound had very little tidal variation. They would either need to be in a boat at the entrance or stand just to the side of the cave on a rock formation. While everyone was looking for a way down to the rock formation, Portagee looked down at his compass. The needle was no longer spinning counter clockwise, instead it was now pointing due north.

Portagee yells, "Guys, look! The compass is pointing due north. I was right. This is a gateway."

No one had noticed, but there was a pair of eyes monitoring the Shark Hole proceedings from high up in a large cedar tree, close enough to see and hear everything. Finally, Bubba tripped and fell and found a pathway that was mostly covered by brush. They cleared out the brush and went down close to the cave's entrance. Spence directed Bubba and Cooter to stand guard and watch for any sign of movement. He then told the Spinners to do whatever they had to do to test the gateway. Michael asked Sam for the cross. While she was passing it over to Michael the hidden observer took note that it was THE cross. Michael then took the cross and at the entrance of Shark Hole raised the cross and faced the emeralds into the hole. The electromagnetic waves began emitting from the entrance and now the cross came alive with the green emeralds forming a triangular laser beam streaming into the entrance. The Spinners all noticed that this laser blast was at a much lower level that the one they had witnessed at the Unfinished Cathedral. In fact, the gateway had opened, but the size of the gateway was only large enough to stick your hand through. Michael instructed Sam to look into the gateway. She saw water and light on the other side. She then slid her arm through quickly and then retracted it.

Sam then said, "Michael move away with the cross."

He did and the gateway closed.

Sam then added, "My arm did get back, I could feel the ocean breeze in the other world plus I could see daylight. It's very evident without a lightening storm we did not have enough power to fully open the gateway. We will just have to wait for a large thunderstorm."

Keno said, "I wish we could let our families on the other side know that we're alive and well."

Everyone sat there in silently, just coming to grips with their overwhelming sense of disappointment.

Finally Spence spoke up, "I think we'd better be heading back now before its gets too late."

All of a sudden Portagee jumped up and said, "Wait a minute. Let's send a message back to the other side."

"Sure…should we call UPS" said Keno.

"No, seriously," said Portagee. "Sam, I know you have paper and a pen in your backpack. You and Michael start writing a message. We'll tie it to one of our cell phones and after entering our world the phone will instantly turn on and the GPS will be located by Graham's GPS phone. Graham will track the phone down and then read the message."

"That sounds superb except for two problems," Michael said. "One, the phone is going to enter our world and land in the water. Secondly, cell phones don't float, so it needs to be waterproof and float."

Sam said, "Wait a minute. I have several plastic hair caps in my backpack; we'll just put the phone in one of them."

Spence said, "Hold on. I saw an old fishnet back on the rocks that must have come from some ship wreck."

He walked down to the rocks and quickly returned with an old fishnet with corks on the edges to make it float.

"Here you go." Spence said as he threw Portagee two decent-sized corks.

Sam added, "Finished our note. Here's what we said Graham we're all O.K. Yes, we are in the Triangle and it looks like we can't make it back through the Shark Hole gateway until there is a powerful lightening storm. Let our families know all is well. If we need to send more messages we'll do it in the same manner, so keep your phone on. Somehow, try to explain this to my father, but ask him to keep it quiet. Thanks. Spinners Portagee, Sam, Keno and Michael".

Sam then handed the note to Portagee to attach to Keno's cell phone. Sam then pulled out one of her plastic caps and passed it over to Portagee. When finished he passed the cell phone to Spence. Spence looked at it and said, "This is a real phone, where's the wire and the phone line."

Portagee says, "Its wireless and has a battery in it."

Spence say, "If you say so."

He then attached the corks to the phone and secured them with the line from the fishnet. Michael then started the process over again. As the gateway re-opened Spence threw the phone through it. There was a sudden green flash and a small blast, then Michael moved the cross away from the entrance and the gateway closed.

"Alright," Spence says, "The phone is through and we better get out of here."

Keno picked up the fishnet and they made their way back to the longboat.

On their way back, Cooter asked Bubba, "I wonder what a cell phone is?"

Bubba says, "Beats me, it looks like something you throw."

The others all smiled and acted like they didn't hear their comments. As they went out of sight of Shark Hole the figure climbed down from the tree. It was Drax's first mate, Hawkins, and he couldn't wait to tell Drax the latest scoop.

By the time the group made it back to the longboat it was almost dark. Spence didn't think it was safe to spend the night away from Spanish Point. The water was still calm and the skies were clear, so he felt it would be safe to row back to the settlement. As they rowed away from shore and glided along the North Shore they saw the large signal fire that their friends at Spanish Point area had started, indicating the way home.

Bubba said, pointing at the bonfire, "There she blows!"

Spence laughed then said, "Bubba that's what you say when you see a whale not a fire."

"Oh," responded Bubba.

It was about nine o'clock when they pulled the longboat on shore. They secured it and hiked up the hill to the others.

Hawkins did not make it back to St. George's until the next morning. He found Captain Drax in the centre of the camp making an example of one of the crew members who was caught stealing a bottle of rum the night before.

"Well Mr. before I pass judgment on you, do you have anything to say in your defense?"

"Oh yes Captain. I'm sorry. It will never happen again. Please forgive me," said the crying crew member.

"You're right about one thing. It will never happen again," replied Drax. He then walked up to the thief, moved to his side and put his arm over his shoulder.

Drax then said, "I do forgive you mate."

The thief then said, "Thank you Drax."

But before he could finish Drax pulled out a dagger from his boot and shoved it

into the side of the thief. The thief then bent over backwards. Drax calmly pulled the dagger back out and used it to slit the man's throat. Drax dropped the limp body on the ground and said, "Cook….. is my breakfast ready?"

He then went over to the table and was served his breakfast. After Drax was done with his breakfast Hawkins went up to him and said: "Captain, I just returned from the Sound and have some information for you."

"Carry on Mr. Hawkins," responded Drax.

Hawkins began: "Well sir, I was hiding in a cedar tree watching the Sound for any unusual activity. By mid-afternoon a group of the Pilgrims entered the shore of the Sound within a stone's throw of me. They had four new very young Pilgrims with them that I have never seen before. They searched around for the longest time and finally uncovered a hole in the rocks by the shore. You won't believe what I have to say next."

"Try me, go on," replied Drax.

Hawkins continued, "One of the young Pilgrims asked another one to hand him the cross. Captain, it was the cross that you had the night in the cave."

Drax jumped up knocking over the table, and then he grabbed Hawkins by the neck and yelled: "The cross! If you're lying I will choke the life out of you right now Hawkins."

"I swear on a dead man's chest, Captain it's true," choked Hawkins.

Drax dropped him to the ground and said, "Tell me more."

67

Hawkins went on to tell him how the green lightening came out of the cross as it did the night of the cave. He went on to tell how the Pilgrims threw a bright metal object into the hole, but did not have a clue why. Then they left. Drax was all smiles now. He thought the cross possessed all the power in the universe. He could be the most powerful pirate in the Seven Seas.

Drax then said, "Mr. Hawkins, we have some serious planning to do. We will take a couple of longboats and visit our friends at Spanish Point. I must get that cross back. Come on Hawkins, let's make ready."

15

SIGNAL FROM THE TRIANGLE

T he last few days had been the loneliest days of Graham's life. All his best friends were missing in the Triangle and nobody believed his story. If only he could talk to his fellow Spinners and help them. Why did he get left behind? He should be with them right now. Just then, his cell phone rang, "Hello," Graham said.

"Graham, it's your father, I was just checking in on you, are you OK?"

Graham replied, "I'm fine. I was just going to go down to the village to mess around."

"That's fine, but keep away from Skinner and his men," replied Graham's dad.

"OK, bye dad," then Graham hung up.

He started to flip the phone closed but happened to notice out of the corner of his eye that the Spinner GPS light was blinking. He couldn't believe his eyes. Keno's cell phone was giving him his location on the island. He tried calling Keno. No answer. But to his amazement Keno's location was still showing up on the phone. Graham now clicked on the location button to see where on the island Keno was. To his surprise the locator said Keno was near Shark Hole and the locator was invariably accurate to within a hundred yards. Graham immediately left the house heading for the St. George's bus

69

station. He could take a bus right over to Shark Hole. As he walked to the bus station he had somebody tailing him, but Graham didn't know it. Cuda was told to keep an eye on Graham and shadow him wherever he went. Cuda stayed just out of sight on his small scooter. Graham reached the bus station and had to wait twenty minutes for his bus to arrive. Then he was off, heading for Shark Hole, with Cuda riding behind him on the scooter.

After arriving at Shark Hole Graham checked the GPS locator and it indicated that the phone was still there, but he could not find it. Graham searched around for Keno, the phone, or someone using Keno's phone for about forty-five minutes without any luck. By chance, he sat down on the stone wall that ran between the road and Harrington Sound itself. As he sat there he turned around to look out over the water and noticed something floating in the water. It was a plastic bag with a couple of corks keeping it afloat. Then, all of a sudden, it dawned on him that the phone might be in that darn bag. He took off his shoes, socks and shirt and jumped into the water to swim toward the floating bag. As he got near it he could tell it was the phone. He grabbed it and swam back to shore. He quickly got his clothes back on, opened up the plastic bag, which he recognized as a shower cap. He opened up the paper that was wrapped around the phone. He read the note quickly: Here's what it said, "Graham we're all O.K. Yes, we are in the Triangle and it looks like we can't make it back through the Shark Hole gateway until there is a powerful lightening storm. Let our families know all is well. If we need to send more messages we'll do it in the same manner, so keep your phone on. Somehow, try to explain this to my father, but ask him to keep it quiet. Thanks. Spinners Portagee, Sam, Keno and Michael".

Graham was shocked. He got off the wall and moved down the road to the bus stop to catch a bus back to St. George's. He only had to wait about five minutes before a bus pulled up. He stepped onto the bus and headed back to St. George's. Cuda had been watching from higher up on a nearby hill. He had seen everything. He had no idea what any of this meant, but he was going to make a dead head trip back to St. George's and inform Tattoo Jack. He got on his scooter and trailed the bus back. By the time Graham got back to St. George's it was still early enough that he figured if he went by the Police Station he might see Inspector Savage. When he got to the Station Graham asked the desk sergeant to see the Inspector. The sergeant told him to take a seat and he would try to locate him. About ten minutes later the Inspector came out to see Graham.

"Welcome Graham, what can I do for you today?" The Inspector said.

Graham replied, "Inspector I need to talk to you privately."

Inspector Savage said, "Graham, let's go into this side room over here and we can talk."

Both went into the room and Savage closed the door. They sat down at the interrogation table and Savage said, "OK, Graham, let's have it."

Graham, in a very nervous voice said: "I'm sure you're going to have a hard time believing this, but it's true."

"Go ahead, I'll believe you," replied Savage.

Graham then told him the story of what happened today.

Graham then said, "Here's the message, please read it. It's in Sam's hand writing."

The Inspector took the note and read it. "Graham we're all OK. Yes, we are in the Triangle and it looks like we cannot make it back through the Shark Hole gateway until there is a large lightening storm. Let our families know all is well. If we need to send more messages we'll do it in the same manner, so keep your phone on. Somehow try to explain this to my father, but ask him to keep it quiet. Thanks, Spinners Portagee, Sam, Keno and Michael".

Savage finished reading the note with tears in his eyes. His heart believed the note, but his mind was reeling. Wiping the tears from his face he looked at Graham and asked, "Graham, did you really found this note as you just explained to me?"

"Yes sir," replied Graham.

Savage was at a loss as to what to say or do. He already knew, absolutely nobody would believe this story. In fact his career would be in jeopardy if he approached his superiors with such a tale. He finally said to Graham, "I honestly cannot believe this note, but I will keep turning over every stone to locate my daughter and her friends. We will be at Shark Hole during the next thunderstorm. In the meantime, keep that cell phone on and keep watching for those blinking lights. Graham, let's go explain everything to your parents, then I'll visit the other families."

 Graham agreed. They got up and left the room.

Cuda entered the Shinbone Pub to find Tattoo Jack very occupied with one of his girlfriends. "Tattoo," stammered Cuda.

Tattoo didn't like to be disturbed when he was with a woman. "What the HELL do you want?" demanded Tattoo.

"Sorry to bother you boss, but I have some news on that rich kid I've been following."

Tattoo sat up, pushed aside the girl and said, "Babe, catch you later, beat it. Now, Cuda, tell me what you saw."

Cuda told Tattoo the whole story including the weird swim in the Sound when the cell phone with a note tied to it was fished out of the water. He also said the kid made a bee line for the Police Station when he returned to St. George's. He was inside the station for about thirty minutes, when he and Inspector Savage came out of the station together and went to the kid's home. After that, the kid stayed home and the Inspector visited a few other houses.

Tattoo replied, "We have to find out what was written on that message. Whatever it was it made the Inspector get off his butt and go talk to other families. Listen, tomorrow you and Sledge follow the rich kid and find out what was on that note. Just make sure when you take him aside that nobody else sees you. I don't want him to be able to identify you later on."

Cuda said, "Right boss."

Tattoo grinned and said, "Beat it! Now I've got to get back to my lady friend."

Cuda left and Tattoo went back to his pleasures.

The next day Graham was walking down Ocean Street on his way to check out what new DVD movies had arrived at the video store. He was lost in his thoughts wondering about what his friends were doing in the Triangle. As he walked by a deserted and run-down house, two arms reached around the wall that he was passing and dragged him behind it. Before he could say or do anything Sledge threw a strong cloth tourist shopping bag over his head. Then Sledge and Cuda dragged Graham into the deserted house. Graham was kicking and swinging his arms trying to escape, but to no avail. The goons were too big for him. When they got him into the house they threw him down on the floor. They tied his hands behind him with a small braided rope. They were careful not to make it too tight because they didn't want to leave any marks on him. They were going to try to scare the living daylights out of Graham to get him to talk, knowing the fact that they were told not to hurt him.

Sledge snarled at Graham, "Listen up kid. If you want to see tomorrow you better answer a few questions for me."

Graham responded, "Go suck on an onion. I'm not telling you anything."

Sledge sat down on Graham's chest making it difficult for him to breathe and said, "Let's try this again...... while I'm still feeling nice. What did that message say on it that you got out of Harrington Sound yesterday?"

Graham flinched. He was shocked that anyone else already knew about the message.

He replied, "I can barely breathe."

Sledge said, "If you don't answer my question you'll soon be taking your last breath."

Graham struggled to speak, "I don't know what you're talking about. I have no message. You can search me."

Sledge pulled out his boning knife and drew it against Graham's throat, just hard enough that he knew Graham would know what might come next.

"Can you feel my knife?" Sledge queried. "I'm about to slit your throat if I don't get some answers quickly, you punk."

Graham was incredibly frightened now and feared for his life, "O. K.," he said, "What do you want to know?" "That's better," Sledge responded. "What was on that note?"

Graham gasped and then started talking, "It was a note from my friends from the Triangle."

"What do you mean from the Triangle?" he quipped.

"I mean the Bermuda Triangle," replied Graham.

"What kind of fools do you take us for," replied Sledge as he added a little more pressure to the blade.

"I swear it's the truth," cried Graham.

Cuda interrupted, "Let the kid talk."

"Go ahead, then, tell us," responded Sledge.

Graham told them what the note said. To make sure they understood it they made Graham repeat the contents of the note twice more. Graham then told them how he gave the note to Inspector Savage.

Sledge said, "If one word of what you said is a lie, we'll be back for you, punk. When we get done with you, you won't even be good shark bait."

"I assure you I'm telling the truth," Graham pleaded.

Cuda kicked him once on his side to make sure Graham remembered the visit. Then they got up without saying a word. There was silence for several minutes. Finally Graham sat up and shook off the bag that was over his head. He looked around. It was fairly dark in the house. He then stood up and walked outdoors. As he walked down the street towards the village, a fisherman noticed Graham and knew he had a problem.

"Son," he said, "Why are your hands tied behind your back, did you escape from the cops?" Graham thought of a quick retort, "No sir, I was robbed by a gang of kids."

The fisherman pulled out his pocket knife and cut away the rope. He then asked if he could do anything for Graham.

Graham replied, "Thanks, I'm O.K.,. I'll go directly to the Police Station and report them."

The fisherman responded, "Very well," and carried on walking.

Graham decided to keep this to himself for fear of reprisals. Besides, he really couldn't tell the Inspector who had done this. He re-composed himself and went into the video store as if nothing had happened.

Cuda and Sledge found Tattoo down on the "Black Shark".

"Well boys, what did you find out?"

Both goons acted nervously, not sure how Tattoo was going to respond to what they had to tell him.

Sledge spoke first, "Tattoo, no matter what you think, this is what happened."

Tattoo said, "Oh damn! What now?"

Cuda and Sledge told Tattoo the whole story, not leaving out any details.

Tattoo, in a bout of disbelief, said, "That kid must have really thought you were suckers."

Sledge reminded Tattoo how they threatened the kid with the knife and how he truly feared for his life.

"O.K. then," Tattoo replied. "Then the next few times we get a thunderstorm, you know where we'll be. The Shark Hole will have plenty of company those nights." Tattoo did still remember what happened on his last visit to the Unfinished Cathedral during the violent thunderstorm.

"Good job guys. It's dinner time. Let's head up to the Shinbone for some grub," Tattoo said. They all left the boat and walked down Water Street towards the Shinbone.

16

SHARKS AND GHOST SHIPS

S tryker was still dismayed and bewildered by the blitzkrieg attack that was perpetrated on him and his men. For days he has had his men on high alert, watching out for spies and invaders. He needed revenge, but on whom? He knew the Pilgrims had a few soldiers and pilots in their ranks, but he didn't think they were capable of executing such a spectacular maneuver. On the other hand he knew the cutthroat Captain Drax and his pirates had the means, but he didn't think they had the brains to do it. Someone was going to pay. He decided to make a surprise attack on the pirates. For good measure, on the way back to the base, he would capture and kill one or two Pilgrims. Now he had to sit down with his Lieutenant and devise a strategy.

The morning began early in Spanish Point. The patrol had got back so late the night before; everyone was tired and decided to wait until the morning to listen to all the details of the trip. Spence told the others the entire story.

When he was finished, Jason commented, "Well, I guess there is a way out of the Triangle that is if throwing a cell phone through a hole in the water counts as a gateway."

Salty asked, "What in hell is a cell phone?"

Spence smiled and replied, "Don't worry Salty. If I tried to tell you, we would be here all day and still might not get it. Just accept the fact that we threw something into Shark Hole and it transitioned out of the Triangle." Salty gave a confused smirk and said, "What the hell is transitioned?" Spence just smiled.

Michael said, "For the gateway to open fully we need an intense thunderstorm."

"That may take awhile. We don't get nasty storms here too often," Buford added.

Jason replied: "We've had many discussions in the past about leaving the island. The longer we're here the less likely any of us would want to return home. All our loved ones are gone now and life as we knew it is a thing of the past."

Jason went on to say: "We consider ourselves as the watch dogs of the Triangle. With the blood thirsty killers at each end of the island, someone needs to be here to help newcomers survive."

Spence added: "Most of the time, we fail at that. It seems, just like you kids did, most survivors arrive at one end of the island or the other. When that happens, most of those poor souls have no bloody hope of surviving."

Jason then continued, "Now that you know where we stand, we will do anything possible to get you out of here, but we could never follow."

Cooter chimed in, "You know damn well we can't go home. Those damn Yankees beat our butts in the big war."

Spence smiled and said, "I think you should be forgiven by now Cooter, but I'm not so sure. The world ought to be ready for you and your cousins."

"Now that we've got all this off our chests, daylight's burning, let's get going. You've all got your chores to do," said Jason as he headed for the look-out post.

Salty now ready to start tackling his lunch said, "You kids need to be careful with that cross. Captain Drax will stop at nothing if he knows you've got it."

Keno said, "Salty may be an old dog, but he's right. It may be a long time before we get another big thunderstorm."

Michael agreed, "Sam, let's see that cross."

Sam pulled it out of her backpack and handed it to Michael. Michael looked at it for a while and scratched his head, then said, "I just don't know. We couldn't simply saw it in half and keep one piece in your backpack and one piece in my pocket. Portagee, you're the creative one, here, catch this, what do you think?"

Portagee caught the cross, after looking at it from every possible angle he exclaimed:

"I have it. See the large emerald in the centre of the cross?"

"Yes, so what!" replied Sam.

Portagee smiled and said, "I'm sure that's the main source of the Triangle, so I'll remove it. Keno hand me your pocket knife."

Keno did just that, then Portagee proceeded by gently and carefully removing the large emerald. "Here you go Michael," Portagee said as he flipped the emerald over to Michael. "Keep that in your pocket-watch pocket in your jeans," Portagee suggested.

"Good idea," responded Michael as he put the emerald in his pocket-watch pocket. Portagee then handed the cross to Sam. She took it and placed it back inside her backpack.

"Clang, Clang, Clang, Clang.'

"What's that noise?" Keno asked.

As Doc, Tom and Lynn ran by, Tom Yelled back, "Jason has spotted a boat or a ship on the North Shore. Come on."

"Let's go," Portagee said as he took off after the others. Keno, Michael and Sam were hot on their heels. When they arrived at the lookout post, Jason was scanning the ocean with his telescope. He then pointed offshore about a mile. There was a small yacht with its main mast broken off just floating in the water.

"This one is ours; we're the only ones on the island who can see it. Maybe there're some survivors on board. Get a crew together to man the longboat and let's get out to the dismasted yacht before she breaks up," Jason demanded.

He then selected Spence, Tom, Buford, Michael and Keno to man the longboat. The crew proceeded down to Clarence Cove where the longboat had been stashed. Spence directed the rowing as the longboat slowly rolled against the waves. As Buford was rowing next to Michael, he could tell this was all new to him.

Buford poked Michael in the side and said, "Well Yankee boy, you having fun yet?"

Michael smiled and said, "Why sure, Billy Bob."

Buford responded, "That's not my name, that's my third cousin's name from Tupelo." Everyone laughed and kept rowing. It was another beautiful day in the Triangle. Keno and Michael were bustin' their butt's rowing. As they approached the crippled yacht Spence ordered them to quit rowing and pull along side the yacht. As they did, Tom and Buford tied the longboat alongside. It was just starting to sink. Michael and Keno had no idea what they might see next.

Once aboard, Spence commanded, "Check the boat out from stem to stern men. See if you can find anyone."

The search didn't take long. The yacht had been deserted for ages. For all the good and beauty in the Triangle, the Triangle she still had a dark and evil side. Spence had the men salvage anything of value. Keno was very hot and during their short rest period he dived into the ocean. Tom was first to hear the splash and turned to see Keno swimming.

He yelled, "Keno the sharks here aren't very friendly. In fact it's almost lunch time. I think you'd better get out."

As Keno was laughing at Tom, he glanced to his side and saw a very large gray black fin cutting through the water heading straight for him.

Jason, Portagee and Sam were stationed at the lookout post watching the events in the ocean develop. While Jason was monitoring what was happening on the dismasted yacht through his telescope, Sam noticed, off to the east, a ship under sail moving toward the sinking vessel. She elbowed Portagee in the side and said, "Look, a sail boat."

Portagee yelled, "Jason, look over there."

Jason startled, swung around with his telescope and got an eye full.

"Look", Jason gestured, "That ship is flying a Jolly Roger on her mast.

"What's that?" asked Portagee.

"Goofball, it's a pirate's flag," responded Sam.

Jason said, "The ship looks small and very old. It must be pretty darn slow. We need to signal the guys to abandon that yacht as soon as possible."

Sam then asked to see the telescope. She focused on the pirate boat, and then said.

"Jason you better get the guys off that boat immediately. The pirates are sailing on an old Bermuda Sloop. That old craft was designed for racing. They don't have anywhere near as much time as you think they do."

She was right. They seemed to be closing the gap rapidly now. Keno was now racing for his life, but the shark was closing quickly. Just as the shark opened his jaws wide and was poised to make Keno his lunch, "Bang", the shark rolled over and sunk out of sight.

Buford said, "Just like shooting ducks in a barrel," then he licked his finger and wiped the sight. By now Michael and Tom were helping Keno onto the yacht. He was exhausted and just collapsed on the deck. While everyone was attending to Keno they heard another "Bang". This time it was back on land. They could barely see three figures at the lookout station jumping and waving, but that was about all. Finally, Spence took out his telescope and could see that Jason pointing off to the east. He then turned around and saw the sloop closing in on them. He also saw Drax looking at him through his telescope.

He quickly collapsed the telescope and yelled, "Pirates ship on the port side. Let's get the hell out of here."

In their haste they failed to notice that the blood-filled waters around them had now attracted ten to twelve more sharks. The sloop was now within musket range.

Drax yelled, "I don't want these Pilgrims to get back to shore. We want their bounty and, who knows, they might have my cross on them."

Everyone except Tom was back on the longboat now. Tom had taken a towel he found on the yacht and opened up the gas tank and soaked it with gas and then stuck it back in the tank. He made a huge Molotov cocktail, then lit the towel and ran for the longboat. Then "Bang", he was hit in the leg by a musket ball. He lost his balance and fell off the opposite side of the yacht. Spence jumped out of the longboat to help Tom, but by the time he got there it was too late. Tom was a goner. Spence turned back for the longboat just barely avoiding being shot himself. He jumped in the longboat and pushed off.

"Row," Spence shouted.

Michael asked, "Where's Tom?"

Spence replied, "We can't help him now."

Drax was undecided……. go for the longboat or the bounty on the yacht? His greed won out. He turned towards the yacht. Just as they pulled alongside the yacht it exploded. Drax was knocked flat on his back and three of his men were thrown overboard. The sharks quickly attacked. Michael and the rest of the crew could hear their desperate screams. They got the longboat to shore before Drax knew what hit him. Drax quickly assessed the damage to the sloop. With most of the sails ripped, he knew he'd better return to St. George's.

He yelled, "Damn you Pilgrims, when I see you next I'll run my hog sticker through you."

He was now wildly swinging his saber in the air.

"Fire at them," he commanded.

The pirates all fired on command. However they were out of range and the musket balls fell harmlessly into the ocean.

Drax then commanded, "Let's get what's left of this ship back to port."

They turned the sloop around and slowly headed back to St. George's.

When the longboat landed, Spence went to Jason to tell him about Tom's fate. They both went to tell Lynn about the loss of Tom. Except for the one on outlook detail and Bubba and Portagee who were instructed to unload the longboat, everyone else spent the rest of the day consoling Lynn. For the relatively short period of time they had to collect goods from the yacht, they ended up with a pretty good boatload. They unloaded a pile of clothing, which was always useful in the Triangle. Tom had siphoned two gallons of gas from the gas tank on the yacht. Gas was always very useful to the Pilgrims. The ship's pantry was still loaded with canned goods and dehydrated food packages. Bubba had never seen foil packets of dehydrated food.

He said, "Is there really chicken in this bag?"

Portagee replied, "Of course, open it up and add water and just like magic you have a chicken dinner."

Bubba laughed and said, "I think you've been eating loco weed."

They also picked up nylon ropes, blankets, life preservers, cooking utensils and other odds and ends. Spence had also found a 22 caliber pistol and three boxes of ammunition. This gave the Pilgrims one of the most modern weapons on the island. Bubba and Portagee finished unloading, and then they packed the goods away carefully. After they were done, they had some fun showing Salty some of the new fangled items to cook with. As far as he was concerned, all he needed was wooden spoons, forks and a butcher's knife.

17

CLAIMED FOR THE FATHERLAND

From his camp on Ireland Island, Stryker had heard the massive explosion of the yacht. He quickly scanned the ocean with his telescope, saw the yacht burning and then watched it founder. He then saw the sloop sailing off towards the east end of the island. Stryker, being a paranoid war monger, knew that some sort of invasion was imminent. After all these years, it was time to attack and eliminate the enemies of the Third Reich. Stryker ordered his men to organize and prepare for an offensive to claim this island for the Fatherland.

"Be prepared to march at sunrise," he commanded.

Stryker was pretty burnt out from everything that had been happening over the past few days.

Every week, Georgette and Lynn made a foraging trip to the central part of the island. The central portion of the island was less unspoiled and was relatively safe for two women and an armed bodyguard to search for fruit, chickens, eggs or whatever else they could find. Lynn was in no shape to go on this week's forage, so Sam volunteered to help Georgette. Sam said she was very familiar with that part of the island that she knew as Devonshire Parish. Jason agreed that it would be alright for her to go on tomorrow's trip and he chose Buford to accompany the ladies.

The next morning they left the settlement shortly after breakfast.

Portagee ran after them yelling, "Be careful. There are lots of wild hogs out there. I hear they have a vicious snort."

Keno and Michael laughed and urged Portagee on.

Sam yelled back, "You make sure you milk those goats while we're gone."

After that they went over the crest of the hill and out of sight.

Cooter then turned to the boys and said, "Well, what are you boys waiting for?"

Portagee responded, "Waiting for what?"

Cooter laughed and said, "To go milk the goats, let's go now."

The boys sighed and followed Cooter to the goats.

As the little foraging group moved toward the centre of the island, they gathered whatever they found in net bags. When the bags were relatively full they hung them from trees and left them. When they could, they would pick them up on the way back or when they arrived back at the settlement they would get help and return to collect all the bags. Today, they were having great luck with Suriname cherries and wild carrots. By mid-afternoon they were well into the centre of the island. Georgette and Sam had talked non-stop. By now, Buford was about to go crazy, he had never heard so much senseless talk in all his life.

He finally said, "You ladies better stop and catch your breath if you plan to make it back today. I'm afraid one of you is going to pass out from lack of breath."

Georgette said, "Why, what in heaven's name do you mean, Buford?"

Buford replied, "What I mean is, if you don't stop talking and inhale...... you're gonna pass out."

Sam said, "Oh don't worry about us. Girls can survive on less air than men."

Buford sighed, "That's great. I think I'll go shoot a hog or maybe just do myself in."

As he walked off through the brush the girls laughed and resumed their foraging and nattering.

This was the second day of the Nazi march across the island. They were in full combat gear, as best they could be, after being on the island for more than fifty years. It was a bizarre sight to see Nazi SS troops carrying muskets and sabers while goose-stepping. The troops looked comical except for the fact that they were cold-blooded killers who were now on a mission to kill anyone or anything that crossed their path. To make time they stayed on the hog trails and marched Indian file. At this point, they cast caution to the wind in order to maintain their fast pace. Buford had heard some noise down in the valley. He knew there were hog trails down there and there might be a small herd of hogs rooting around. In this part of the island they were not hunted very often so they did not have much to fear. Buford knew he was still far from the trails, but as he got closer, the sounds the hogs were making seemed odd. It reminded him of something, but he just couldn't work it out. As he started closing the gap he became more obsessed with the sound. He guessed the noise was something he remembered from his days back in the other world, but he couldn't place it. Meanwhile the girls were enjoying themselves. It was a perfect day, and they occasionally were side-tracked when they found gorgeous wild flowers covering the small hills. Georgette told Sam it was moments like these when she forgot her past life and called this beautiful island her paradise home.

Georgette laughed and said, "You know I just may choose to live here forever."

Sam smiled and thought to herself how much she already missed her home and family and wondered if she was ever to return.

Sam then said, "Where did Buford go, I thought he was supposed to stay with us?"

"Well," Georgette responded, "Buford's an old hunter and every now and again he forgets what he's supposed to be doing. If he gets the scent of a wild hog, you may not see him for hours. When you hear a shot or two you know he'll be on his way back, with or without a hog strapped to his back." Sam set aside her concern and started picking some flowers.

Buford was getting closer to the trails and now he was in his hunting fever. The sound was still gnawing at the back of his mind, but he kept suppressing it. He was now within a few feet of a trail and it was the one he reckoned the hogs were coming down. He waited till they got closer. Then, he planned to jump out on the trail, take aim at the lead hog and drop it dead in its tracks. Closer and closer they came. He just couldn't wait any longer. Just as he leaped through the bushes he realized what that familiar sound was:

"Union Soldiers!"

It was too late now he was in the middle of the trail pointing his musket barrel straight at Stryker. His reflexes kicked in and he fired. In the split second that he fired, one of the Nazi SS Troopers shoved Stryker aside to get a shot at Buford and was instantly shot through the heart. He dropped dead. Before Buford could move Stryker spun back around with his saber drawn and ran it through Buford's side. Buford doubled over and fell backwards. Stryker tried to finish Buford off with another swing of his saber. Valiantly, Buford managed to block the saber with his musket, the blade imbedding itself into the musket and when Stryker pulled back, the musket was ripped out of Buford's hand. Buford then turned and cart rolled head-first through the bushes. He got to his feet and started running even though he was in excruciating pain. By now, several of the Nazi SS Troopers were running after him to finish him off. Buford jumped through another row of bushes, tripped and rolled down the hillside. Half way down he rolled over a protruding stone ledge and fell straight down into a crevice.....out of sight. When he hit bottom he cracked his head on the side of the stone crevice and passed out. The Nazi SS Troopers ran through the bushes and when they came out, they stopped and looked down the hill. From their perspective, it looked like the stone ledge was the bottom of the hill and they saw nothing of Buford. They about-faced and went on. The girls had heard the shots from far off in the distance.

Georgette said, "See! I told you he'd find some hogs. It sounded like he missed with the first shot and had to shoot a second time. He hates to have to fire a second round. We'll have to tease him when he gets back. He ought to be a better marksman."

Sam was concerned. She commented, "Those two shots were too close together to have come from the same musket. He could never have reloaded his gun that fast."

The smile on Georgette's face left very quickly and she burst out, "Oh my God, we can't loose another member of our family."

They both agreed they should go in the direction of the shots and try to locate Buford. As they got closer, the trail they were on, split into a Y. Georgette took the left trail and Sam chose the right. For safety sakes they agreed to be as quiet as possible and not call for Buford. The plan was to return to the Y after thirty minutes, with or without Buford.

The SS Troopers returned to the hog trail without Buford. They reported that they had lost him in the woods. Stryker was visibly upset but was comforted by the knowledge that with such a wound the soldier would soon die anyway. His little army was down to seven SS Troopers plus himself. They couldn't suffer any more losses, so they slowed down and began to move more carefully down the hog trail. Stryker was now convinced something big was about to happen. Was the war finally coming to this lost island? He was ready to claim the island for the Fatherland or go down in glory trying to prevent the Allies from occupying the island. Stryker ordered one of his SS Troopers to move ahead and scout out the terrain in front of them. The SS Trooper, who had just been shot at, was being extremely cautious. He was not going to be taken off guard again. He was about a hundred yards ahead of the rest of the troops, when he thought he heard something coming down the trail towards him. His first hunch was that it was a couple of wild hogs, and if it was, he knew what he'd be eating that night. The SS Trooper moved off the trail just in the dense growth, cocked the hammer back on his musket and waited. He didn't have long to wait. Within minutes an unsuspecting Sam came walking down the trail. She was being very careful to be on the lookout for Buford. As she got within a few yards of the SS Trooper she saw the musket barrel sticking out of the growth. Sam knew all was not well. She slowly turned and started walking in the other direction.

Before she got 10 paces the SS Trooper jumped out of the growth and yelled, "Halt, or I'll shoot."

When Sam heard his voice she started a dead run, but it was too late. The SS Trooper lunged at her and just grabbed her ankle. Sam, with her ankle in his vise-like grip fell and slightly twisted her ankle. She tried to get up, but the SS Trooper kept her pinned to the ground.

Sam screamed, "Let me go."

But the SS Trooper lay there on top of her, staring at her. Sam began to fear what might happen next. Impulsively she kneed him in the groin. He screamed bloody murder, clutched for his privates and rolled over into a ball.

As quickly as she could, Sam got up to run, but at that moment a large hand grabbed her and said, "I see we meet again, my little fraulein."

Sam yelled, "Let me go you oaf."

Meanwhile Georgette had heard the scream and decided to cut across the wooded area from one trail to the other. As she neared she saw that Sam had been captured by the Nazis. She realized the situation was hopeless for the moment, so she watched and waited.

Stryker was all smiles, he said, "My pretty little one, what are you doing out in the woods by yourself?"

Sam did not say a word, just stared at him in disgust. The one-eyed Nazi decided to heat things up a little.

"Well, you are alone now. We just shot and killed your soldier friend."

Sam screamed, "You murderer."

She then raised her hand in an attempt to slap him, but before her hand struck, Stryker seized her wrist and almost bent it in half. Sam screamed with pain. Georgette winced in sympathy and accidentally her foot snapped a twig.

Stryker looked up and barked, "What was that? You two go check it out. But just as they were starting off, an old turtle meandered out on the trail.

Stryker then said, "Never mind: it was nothing."

As he looked at Sam he noticed her backpack, he grabbed it and almost pulled Sam's arms out of their sockets trying to get it off.

"Hold her, while I look at her backpack," he commanded.

Stryker dug through the backpack not finding anything of interest at first. Then he saw the glistening golden cross.

Stryker smiled and said, "Look what I have. A lovely golden cross with emeralds. A pity it's missing one. Do you have any more jewels, pretty one?"

Sam replied, "No and that's not yours, you thief."

Stryker was distressed by her accusation and said: "You better shut your mouth before I shut it permanently."

He then took the cross and strung it through the chain he had been wearing around his neck and then hung it around his neck.

"Yes, the spoils of war," Stryker explained. "Tie her hands behind her back and let's get moving," Stryker commanded.

They were now off again with their prisoner of war.

When the Nazis cleared the curve in the trail and she could no longer see them, Georgette made a move to return to the settlement. It was clear the Nazis were not heading back to their camp, plus they had backpacks and rolled up blankets attached to them. They must be planning to be away from their camp for awhile with all the supplies that they carried with them. Then Georgette started crying. She just remembered Stryker had said he had killed Buford. Her only option was to slip back to the settlement as quickly as she could, to get help.

Buford was coming around slowly. He woke up and found himself encased in a stone pit. For a minute he thought he was back at the Battle of Bull Run where he found himself buried in a trench with explosions all around him. Eventually, his senses returned and he realized his predicament. Buford rolled over and could see he might have a chance to crawl out of the crevice. He knew his side was bleeding and unless he could crawl out quickly he might bleed to death. Buford was a survivor. He inched his way out of the crevice after about thirty minutes. Once out into the open, he had a chance to examine his wound. It all happened so fast he wasn't sure if he had been shot or stuck with a hog sticker. It was the latter. Buford removed his shirt and covered his wound with it. He then wrapped his belt around his upper waist to hold the make shift bandage on. He knew he had to get back to where the girls were to warn them. He was totally unaware of what had already taken place.

Buford figured it was now safe to go back to the trail. He found his chopped up musket lying in the bushes. It turned out to be a very good crutch to help him walk back towards where he had left the girls. As Buford entered the clearing, he heard a woman crying.

Buford bleated, "Georgette, is that you?"

Georgette perked up and went running towards the sound. When she saw Buford she said, "The Nazis told me that they'd killed you."

"Na, I'm too tough to let a hog sticker be the end of me," Buford responded. Then he dropped to the ground in pain. "Don't worry I'll be able to recover," Buford managed.

Georgette ran over to help him. She said, "Let's rest here for awhile."

Buford agreed and while they rested they told each other what had happened.

It was beginning to get late in the afternoon and Spence realized the foraging group was overdue. They never stayed out after dark. It was too dangerous with the pirates and Nazis wandering around. The group agreed it was time to send out a search party for Buford, Georgette and Sam. Jason picked Spence, Bubba and Keno to send out. Spence and Bubba were issued a musket and Keno a saber. They also took wooden torches to light, if they had to keep searching after dark. Bubba was specially chosen because he was a good tracker. As expected, he found the trail early on. They soon came across the first bag of fruits and vegetables hanging from a tree branch.

Spence said, "Good job Bubba. We know they got this far and they've not turned back yet or they would have retrieved this bag."

The search party went on. In the meantime, Georgette and Buford were slowly heading directly towards the search party.

The Nazis had been making very good time…even dragging Sam along. Stryker's goal was to finish the day at a small bay that had a large rock overhang. There they would be able to camp below the overhang for protection from the weather and any enemies. For anybody to attack them there, they would have to come straight across the sandy beach. Just before dark, they reached the bay which was very familiar to Sam. She knew it as John Smith's Bay. It was one of the nicest beaches on this side of the island. She never dreamed she would visit this beach under such circumstances. While her cutthroat captors were busy making camp, Sam, for a few moments, was caught up in her thoughts and dreams. Sam quickly re-focused as they started a large fire up under the rock ledge which faced towards the ocean. The fire was well concealed from land. The Nazis began to roll out their blankets for the night and were eating some of the fruits and dried meat they had brought with them. One of the SS Troopers handed Sam some dry meat and a prickly pear to eat. The same guy also threw her the blanket that had belonged to the SS Trooper that Buford had shot and killed that day. Sam thanked him, but all he did was grunt back at her and walk away. Stryker was sitting by the fire, across from Sam, admiring his repossessed golden cross. As he spun it in his fingers, the brilliance of the gold and emeralds cast a glow that bounced around the surrounding rock walls.

He looked at Sam and said, "Some day when I get back to the Fatherland, this cross will make me a very rich man. Don't you think so, pretty one?"

Sam replied, "If you're not careful it might be the end of you."

Stryker laughed, and then added, "You and your pilgrim friends are a bunch of inferior ingrates. I have no fear of you. We are the superior race, destined to rule the world for a thousand years."

Sam already knew his one thousand year empire would only last for about fifteen years, but she decided that keeping silent might be the right thing to do. She had already witnessed his ugly temper. With that, she turned around and lay down wrapped up in her blanket. Stryker, getting no response, commanded one of the SS Troopers to give him one of the old bottles of rum that they had found on an old shipwreck. He took the bottle and chugged down some rum while he continued to spin his cross.

It was now dark and the search party had ignited their torches to see their way down the trail. They maintained about a ten pace distance from each other just in case they ran into the Nazis or pirates. With this distance, two of the three would have a chance to defend themselves and escape. Keno was in the middle.

As they walked he asked, "Has it always been this dangerous here?"

Bubba responded, "No, only since you kids arrived."

"Bubba's pulling your leg. It comes and goes around here. Lately it's been a little intense, but don't worry we'll find our buddy," Spence offered.

"Thanks," Keno replied.

They went on quietly down the winding trail, listening and keeping a weather eye out for their companions.

Georgette and Buford had stopped to rest for awhile. Buford's loss of blood was taking its toll on him and without some immediate medical attention, he might not survive.

Georgette pleaded, "Come on Buford, get up. We have to get back to the others."

Buford blurted: "Go on, get the Hell out of here and save yourself. I'll be alright. You can come back for me tomorrow with the others."

Georgette retorted: "Get your big Johnny Reb butt up now. I'm not taking no for an answer. I'll drag your sorry ass back if I have to." She then stood up and grabbed Buford by the arm and started pulling him up.

"OK, OK, I get the message. You're trying to kill me now," Buford grimaced in pain.

Finally they pulled together and started hobbling up the trail. They had moved about thirty feet when Georgette saw a burning light further up the trail. A minute later she saw another burning light and then shortly afterwards she saw yet another.

"Buford," she said, "I think that's a search party looking for us."

Buford replied, "Let's make sure. Let's move off the trail and watch for a while."

They hobbled off the trail and sat down in the bushes.

As Spence, Keno and Bubba walked by, Buford asked, "Anyone got a light?"

The all froze in their tracks, then looked around and saw Georgette and Buford sitting in the bushes.

Bubba said, "Now, did you all ever see such a pretty sight?" As Georgette helped get Buford to his feet, the rest of them could see he was hurting.

Bubba went over to him and asked, "What happened, did you shoot yourself?"

"Very funny, our good friend Stryker stuck me with a hog sticker, but I took out one of his henchmen first."

Spence said, "You're lucky they didn't kill you, you big baboon."

About then Keno panicked, "Where's Sam? I don't see Sam."

Georgette responded, "Stryker abducted her, she appears to be O.K."

Spence said, "I fear for her. Plus he now possesses the key to the gateway."

Keno said, "Don't worry about that. Yesterday we removed the large central emerald from the cross, and we're pretty sure no one can use it now."

"Well by golly, at least that's good news," replied Bubba.

Spence said, "We have to get Buford back to the settlement as quickly as possible, then tomorrow we'll head out to rescue Sam."

With that Spence and Bubba found two strong cedar saplings and chopped them down with their sabers. The three men took off their shirts and split the necks open to the sleeves. They then took the saplings and ran one on each side of the shirts. Tying the sleeves together under the back of the shirt they were able to make a surprisingly sturdy stretcher on which to put Buford. Buford lay down on the stretcher and Bubba picked up the back end and Keno picked up the front. Spence led the group, carrying a torch in one hand and a musket in the other. Georgette brought up the rear also carrying a torch and two muskets strapped to her back. As they passed the hanging bags of fruit and vegetables, Spence cut them down so the animals and birds could feed on them. He knew they could not get back for them and did not want them to go to waste. Even carrying the stretcher, they were able to return to the settlement in the early morning hours. Buford was immediately taken to Doc for medical attention. The rest of the group huddled together for a short while to discuss what had happened. They decided to get a few hours of shut-eye, and then meet after dawn to plan the rescue strategy.

Sam awoke just in time to see the sun rise over the ocean. It was another cloudless day in paradise. Then she came back to reality and overheard Stryker planning the day's travel route with his SS Troopers. She got up and went over to the fire. Most of the SS Troopers had already eaten, but there were still a few pieces of hogfish left on the wood sticks leaning over the fire coals. Sam helped herself and sat down to listen in on the plans. The Nazis appeared not to care whether she was listening. They figured she wasn't a threat. Stryker appeared to be obsessed with the idea of invading the East end of the island. Sam thought he had snapped because he was convinced that a Nazi invasion was eminent. Stryker drew the map in the sand as he was talking.

"Listen men," he said. "This morning we will stay on this coast line until we get past the second of the little lakes. Then we will move in a northeasterly direction up between the area that has the sound on one side and the large bay on the other side. Remember, stay away from the sound coastline. Drax may have his spies out. Then, we will move up and cross the water, on to the tiny island. From there we will be able to move over to the western tip of Drax's island. There they could spend the night and prepare for the attack the next day. Sam knew that they were going up by the caves she knew and on to cross the water at Coney Island, then over to Ferry Reach. She prayed that Drax would be on the high ground and would easily be able to see these war mongers coming, long before they reached St. George's. She knew that Drax and his pirates, though not crazy like the Nazis, were just as ruthless and might need to try to escape sometime today. The problem was she didn't want to leave without the cross. If Drax got his hands on the cross they would have to kill him to get it back or never go home again. Stryker ended the meeting by standing up, clicking the heels of his boots together and giving the Nazi salute. The SS Troopers moved around the camp packing up, like little army ants. Within twenty minutes they were ready to break camp and move out.

While the Nazis were on the move again the Spinners and their new-found family were beginning to congregate in Spanish Point. Bubba and Cooter carried Buford out to the group in the make-shift stretcher. When they arrived, Doc assured them that Buford was as tough as nails and would survive.

Jason started off by saying, "It appears that the Nazis are headed for the St. George's Island because they did not return to their camp last night. If they were heading our way we would have been attacked last night or this morning. I have no idea what they're up to, but Buford said last night they were in uniform and fully armed. Something has triggered them to lash out like this. I'm sure we had something to do with it when we took them by surprise to free and save our young friends. Maybe the yacht explosion also had something to do with it. At any rate they must have thought Drax and his pirates were behind these actions. Anyway, we don't mind if these two groups of thugs and henchmen kill each other off, but we do need to rescue Sam and recover the cross if we can. Stryker and his men are a day ahead of us assuming they are going this way to the East end."

He then pulled out his old flight map and pointed out the way he thought they were going.

Spence added, "If Stryker has snapped and is careless, Drax will do him in. The problem is that we can't catch up to him, even by longboat. So my guess is that we're going to have to deal with the aftermath of the collision of the two factions. We will then have the same problem as Stryker, how to get to St. George's Island without being noticed." Michael then stood up and said, "I've got an idea." He then took the map. "Let me show you," he continued. "If we cross over by Shark Hole and continue along the southern coastline we can cross through what we know as Tucker's Town in the south. We can then swim from island to island across the opening of the harbour, and we will end up here," pointing at St. David's. "We won't be noticed. Drax will be occupied off the North Shore and will never expect us to arrive from the south. From there, we can swim to Paget Island and then over to St. George's. The element of surprise is worth all that swimming. Furthermore, Keno and Portagee know The East end inside out."

Michael then sat down.

Jason commented: "I think we all need to salute you Michael and dub you General Michael. That's an incredible game plan to get us in the back door without being noticed. Now all we have to do is figure out what to do when we get there. Unfortunately, we may not know that answer until we get there and see who is still standing. At any rate, the day is getting away from us. We need to get ready to get going as soon as possible. I think everybody knows what we have to do to prepare. Any questions?"

None were asked.

Spence responded, "Good, let's get moving and while you're getting ready, Jason and I will choose who is to go. Thanks."

All the preparation was done in about an hour. Everyone was hanging around waiting for their assignments. Jason addressed the group: "Spence and I have added a new twist to the rescue operation. We are now going to have two assault plans operating independently. The first mission is still General Michael's plan. However, we're also going to try a quicker but more dangerous mission. Spence and another of you will rig up our longboat with a mast and that pair will sail along the North Shore. This sailing duo has a chance to catch Stryker either at Coney Island or after they cross to Ferry Reach. This should be well before they reach Drax and his pirates. They will probably have to sail all night and make a night landing in order to not be noticed. At any rate, it's a long shot but we need to chance it. Should they be too late or they never get an opportunity to rescue Sam they will simply stay concealed and try a rescue after the fighting starts or when they see an opportunity arise. Since Spence has never been to that part of the island we are hoping one of the Spinners will volunteer for the sailing mission. Any volunteers?"

All three of the boys raised their hands.

Spence said, "That's great, but I only need one of you. Who is the best sailor?"

Portagee spoke up first, "I am. Not only do I know that part of the island as well as the others, but I am much handier on a boat. I grew up on my father's fishing boat."

The other two couldn't dispute that point with Portagee and conceded to him.

"Well then," replied Jason, "It's settled. Portagee will go with Spence for the overnight sailing approach. Now let's all get down to the longboat and rig up a mast."

Cooter then stopped the group, "But then who's going on the General's mission?"

Jason replied, "Good question. Since Bubba and Cooter are the most experienced wielding weapons they will go. But for guides, Michael and Keno will join them. We know Keno knows the St. David's area like the back of his hand. You two will carry sabers for protection, but won't expect you to join the fight. That leaves Georgette, Lynn and Doc to hold the fort down here and of course, Buford, you can protect them from your stretcher... just kidding. Any questions?"

Lynn answered, "Yes, why can't I go. I want to avenge Tom.."

"I understand your feelings, but now's not the time for vengeance, we need clear thinkers. You'll get a chance later.

Salty had kept quite until now, "Look here Lynn, I'm too old to go after any of those rum–sucking, back-stabbing baboons. Someone's got to stay and keep me company."

Lynn did not agree, but she always tolerated Salty.

"Alright you old swashbuckler, I'll stay and make your life miserable," replied Lynn. Salty smiled and winked as he gave Lynn a hug.

"Let's all get down to the cove and get the boat rigged," Jason said.

Two hours later the longboat was ready to go. Spence and Portagee climbed on board and the others gave them a shove off. Jason and the others waved to them as they rowed out of the cove.

Jason called after them, "God speed."

But by then Spence and Portagee were out of earshot and did not hear them. Jason and the others went back up the hill to load up and hit the trail as they had lots of ground to make up. Jason and the others picked up their weapons, backpacks and life preservers to cross the inlet and left the settlement. The girls closed the gates. Lynn went to the lookout post and Georgette went to check on Buford. Jason's group stuck to the North shore coastline. It was their intention to maintain this course until they reached

Flatt's Inlet. Then they would circle the south shoreline of the Sound until they made it to the area Michael called Shark Hole. Then they would head on south to the South Shore coast. The pace was fast, but they were all young and fit so they were able to make good time. The longboat was far enough away to take advantage of the wind so Portagee hoisted the sail and the small craft picked up speed. Spence was impressed with Portagee's ability to handle the longboat. He was glad Portagee spoke up to be part of this mission. In almost no time at all, they were approaching Flatt's Inlet. Portagee noticed the weather was changing. The skies were darkening and the wind was picking up. The waves were building and Portagee commented that it looked like they might be in for gale force winds that night. This was a good news/bad news development. The good news; if they stayed out in the ocean for a while longer, they could double their speed. Plus with the waves getting higher Stryker might not be able to cross over to Coney Island and on to St. George's for several hours. The bad news was that Jason's team would not be able to island-hop to St. David's from Tucker's Point for the same reason. The worst of the bad news was that if Spence and Portagee stayed out too long in the rough waters they might easily sink. Spence wished he could communicate with Jason. If Stryker got stuck on the North shore it might pay for Jason's team to turn north past the lakes and surprise them from the rear. That was wishful thinking. He had no idea what was going through Jason's mind just then.

Stryker was now just about a half mile away from the North Shore. The wind was picking up and the rain was starting to pelt down. It was blowing so hard the rain was almost horizontal, which made it very difficult to see. They pushed on. It was late afternoon and because of rapid approach of the heavy storm, it was getting dark and seemed much later than it actually was. By the time the Nazis made the North Shore the waves were cresting higher than two feet, which was high for the island. The Nazis and Sam stood on the water's edge looking over at Coney Island. Most of the men were worried about trying to swim over, especially since half of them had no flotation devices of any kind. Stryker was so obsessed that he threw caution to the wind and ordered his men to start swimming to Coney Island.

He turned to Sam and said, "You go first pretty one, unless you'd prefer a bullet in your head."

He signaled one of his SS Troopers to aim his musket at her. Sam thought for a moment to run... the powder in the muskets was probably wet and would not fire, but she couldn't be sure. She was an excellent swimmer. In fact she was sure she could reach the island, but wondered if the Nazis could, loaded down with muskets and equipment fighting the rough water. Sam jumped in the water and started swimming for her life. She never looked back: she just fought the waves and current to avoid being swept into the harbor. Stryker quickly commanded his men to follow and, like little toy soldiers, they went in, one by one. Stryker was the last to go, but he was the one with the life preserver and no equipment weighing him down. Everyone lost sight of one another and were swimming desperately trying to save their lives. It took the group about ten minutes to get across the small channel to the island. Once there and near exhaustion, Stryker took a head count. One of the SS Troopers was missing. They presumed he had drowned or was swept out into the harbor. Sam just sat there thinking what a mad man she was with. The Nazis made their way over to the other side of the tiny island, to survey the sea's conditions, in order to get on over to the main East end island. The waves were now three to five feet high and even the mad man Stryker knew it would be suicidal to try to continue in the gale.

Stryker then commanded, "Make camp here for the night. Make or find the best shelter you can for the night. We'll continue in the morning."

Jason's team had just passed the second lake, they were at the same turning point that Spence had turned north before. Jason, for a moment or two, thought that Stryker might be stuck on the North shore, but then again, what if he had reached the North shore before the storm hit? He decided to stay the course and head on out to Tucker's Point to check out the waves.

About an hour later they made it to the tip of Tucker's Point, when they realized that with these three to five foot waves blasting through the harbour, they would be swept out to sea before making the first small island. Jason told the team to make camp as best as they could. They would wait and see what tomorrow would bring. As they sat around getting soaked, they were worried about Spence and Portagee as to whether or not they had made it to shore safely. They also felt that Stryker by now was also bogged down.

Spence and Portagee had taken full advantage of the storm and used the strength of the wind to almost catch up with Stryker. Portagee was now afraid that maybe they had pushed too hard and that they were going to sink before they could make it to shore. It was almost dark now, and Spence and Portagee agreed they needed to make it to shore. They were just at the tip of North shore and could barely see Coney Island. They could see movement on the south side of the tiny island. It looked like they were trying to hunker down and use the rocks to hide behind for shelter from the storm approaching from the north. Spence pointed to the island and asked Portagee, "That has to be Stryker because Drax and his men wouldn't be caught dead in a storm like this. Is there a place on the north side of the island to land without being seen?"

Portagee replied, "Yes on the northeast side there is a very small spot where we can land."

"Good, let's go for it," said Spence.

They dropped the sail and started rowing for that bay. They didn't have to worry about making too much noise as the wind was howling. The waves were crashing on the island and there was plenty of thunder booming around. Because of the horizontal rain coming in from the north, the Nazis weren't looking in that direction, so they did not have to worry about being seen. Plus, who would expect visitors on a night like this?

Spence and Portagee made it to the island and landed where they had planned. They pulled the battered longboat up on shore as best as they could. Portagee knew that the Nazis must be within fifty feet from where they had landed, so they crawled very slowly and carefully over the rocks trying to reach a vantage point to see if they could find Sam. After staying in their vantage point for about ten minutes, A lightning bolt struck. Portagee saw a glimmer of the cross and instantly thought it was Sam. He pointed in that direction for Spence to see. Portagee started to crawl down the rock toward the figure with the cross and just then, Spence saw some long hair blowing in the wind ten feet in the other direction. He reached down quickly, and at the last second, was able to grab Portagee's shoe and stop him. He was about to get himself killed. Portagee backed up and Spence pointed towards Sam. He signaled to Portagee that he could slip down to her and he needed to watch his backside. Spence slid down the rocks until he was just above Sam. He quietly reached down with both hands and quickly covered her mouth to keep her from making a noise that would alert the others.

Sam just about jumped out of her skin. She started to kick and fight back, but then Spence whispered, "It's me, Spence."

Sam stopped struggling. Spence pulled back his hand and reaching down, grabbed Sam's arm and pulled her up to the top with him. He then signaled for her to follow him.

When they got back to where Portagee was, Sam said, "Thanks - but Stryker has the cross." Spence whispered back, "we'll have to worry about that some other time.'

As they started to move back to the longboat, Portagee slipped and fell over some rocks.

The next thing they heard was, "Who goes there?"

Then they heard, "The girl's missing."

They started running toward the longboat. Sam and Portagee made it to the boat, but just as Spence approached the boat, a Nazi SS Trooper tackled him and knocked him over on the rocks. A fight ensued. They were rolling all over the rocks, when a stern voice enunciated, "Stop, if you want to live." Spence and the SS Trooper stopped fighting. Then Spence looked around and saw five SS Troopers with muskets pointing at him.

Stryker then said, "Get out of that boat with your hands over your head!"

Portagee and Sam started to follow the orders, and then Spence held his hand up and stopped them. He winked back at the Spinners and turned around and cold cocked the SS Trooper he was fighting with his fist.

He then looked up at Stryker and said, "Auf Wiederschen," then smiled and jumped in the boat and said, "Push off quickly."

Just then Stryker screamed, "Fire!"

All you heard were five clicks as the triggers were pulled. The gun powder was wet as Spence expected. He also knew they were too far away from him to stop him after they figured their muskets wouldn't fire.

As they were whisked away to the south by the waves, Sam yelled, "You're a genius," then hugged him for saving her.

Portagee sighed, "What about me? I saved you too."

She then turned around and hugged him.

Sam then said, "What now?"

Portagee pointed in the direction that they were being whisked, "We're on a direct course to Tucker's Point. We'll be safe there."

Spence added, "I think we'll find our friends there also. So let's get this poor old wreck under control and make land."

They were being carried so fast by the wind and waves that the longboat was being pulled to the east towards the other harbor entrance.

Spence yelled, "Portagee, put everything you have in it. If we miss Tucker's Point, we'll find ourselves hundreds of miles out to sea."

Portagee was already rowing as hard as he could, and they were slowly moving back towards the point. The waves had other ideas - crashing over the boat and bouncing it around like a cork. The boat was taking on water faster than Sam could bail. Then they heard the planks on one side of the boat snapping like toothpicks. They had just struck some jagged rocks close to shore when the longboat spun around and struck a huge second rock. All the crew could do was to just hang on for their lives, because if they were thrown into the ocean here, they would be sliced to pieces by the jagged rocks. A rogue wave picked up the longboat, shoved it over the rocks and threw it on the beach. Spence, Portagee and Sam quickly jumped out of the boat and pulled it as far up the beach with what strength they had left.

Tomorrow, weather permitting, they would drag the longboat over to see if it could be saved. Now they had to get up over the crest of the hill behind them. Hopefully, on the other side, they would find some protection from the rain and wind. If they were lucky they might also find their friends.

Stryker was furious. He had just lost his hostage and couldn't do anything about it. He turned around cursing at himself and returned to his sheltered spot, where he would spend the rest of the night obsessing over tomorrow's events.

Back in the other world the storm was also raging. Graham was in his estate and he heard a car horn sounding outside the gate. He looked out the window and saw the two flashing red lights of a police car. He realized that it was Inspector Savage who was there to pick him up to go to Shark Hole. They had already decided that if there were any nasty storms they would go to Shark Hole in hopes that the Spinners would find their way back through the triangle gateway. Graham made his way out to the car. The Inspector reached over and pushed open the passenger door for Graham.

"Graham, are you ready to find your friends tonight?" the Inspector asked.

Graham jumped in the car and said, "Yes sir." As he closed the door he asked, "Are we going to have the siren on and the lights flashing?"

The Inspector laughed and said, "No. I really don't want to draw any attention to us. I only had the lights flashing so you could see me."

He then turned the flashing lights off and started down the road to Queen Street and back to the village. As they drove on out of St. George's, the streets were all but empty. Not many cared to venture out in this storm. With one exception, Tattoo Jack and Sledge had been following the Inspector that night, knowing something might be going on. Tattoo was staying a very safe distance behind the Inspector. After all, they already knew where they were headed.

Sledge asked Tattoo while he was driving, "Do you really believe this bloody storm boss?" Tattoo snarled back, "All I know is that they have my cross. Whatever it takes I'll get my cross back and I don't care if I have to kick the Governor's royal ass to get it."

"I get the message," replied Sledge.

Tattoo lit up his Cuban cigar, sat back and relaxed as Sledge followed the Inspector.

The Inspector and Graham did not have a lot to say while they were driving to Shark Hole, they both just seemed to be lost in their thoughts. By the time they arrived at Shark Hole the storm was really kicking up. The Inspector pulled over in the bus lay by as the buses were finished running for the night. Plus, who was going to bother a police car? They both got out of the car and went down to where Graham had found the cell phone floating. After waiting for over an hour, both were soaked and very disappointed, to say the least.

The Inspector finally asked, "Graham, is this just BS? Why is there no sign of them tonight?" Graham, trying to maintain a positive twist on this bad situation replied, "Maybe the weather was too bad tonight. Plus there was not a lot of lightning tonight. We really don't know what's happening on their side of the gateway. At any rate Sir, every day or night for the rest of the summer I will be down here waiting. I will never abandon my friends."

The Inspector put his arm around Graham's shoulder and said, "Sam and the others could never ask for a better friend than you. Let's give it up tonight before we catch our death of cold." Graham agreed. They went back to the car and they drove back to St. George's without a single sign from the Spinners that night.

About two hours later a large lighting bolt struck across the sky, followed by a monstrous thunder boom. Sledge and Tattoo were jarred from their nap. They had both fallen asleep and had not seen the Inspector and Graham leave.

Tattoo started yelling, "What the hell just happened? Where did the police car go?"

Sledge just sat there in a daze.

Tattoo slapped him on the back of the head and said, "Get this truck going. We just wasted our night and we don't have a clue if they found anything or not. You let us fall asleep."

Sledge just looked at Tattoo and sighed. He started up the truck and went back to the Shinbone for the rest of the night.

Soaking wet and exhausted, Spence, Portagee and Sam reached the far side of the little peninsula. The weather was still nasty, but at least it was less windy there on the south side. They walked out to the tip of the peninsula but saw no sign of Jason's team. There was no way to tell if the team had already been there or was still on its way. Portagee told Spence that if they

went back down the coastline they would find an overhanging cliff near the beach that would give them shelter for the rest of the night. Spence agreed, as he was fed up with being soaked. They headed down the coastline for about fifteen minutes until they came across the spot Portagee had been talking about. The shelter area was pitch black so they found the driest area they could and laid down to rest.

Then out of the darkness came a voice, "Ya'll make yourselves at home now ya hear," said Cooter.

Spence sat up and said, "You old gun runner. I'm going to kick your butt for scaring the crap out of me."

To everyone's surprise they were all safe and unharmed, especially Sam. After hugs and pats on the back, Spence told the story of the night's events. Jason ordered everyone to get a little shut eye before sun up. They would discuss what to do tomorrow. With that, everyone tried to make themselves as comfortable as possible and tried to drift off to sleep.

The gale had passed in the early morning hours, and now the winds and waves were calming down. Jason and Spence had already been over to the other side of the point to check on the longboat. It was still there, but minor repairs needed to be made to make it seaworthy again. By the time they returned to the cliff overhang, the rest of the group were up and about.

"O.K. everyone, we've got a lot to talk about this morning," Jason said. "Last night was an incredible night for Spence, Portagee and Sam. We're lucky to have them with us again. Stryker tried to kill them but failed. Then the gale tried to wipe them out but it too failed. We had two objectives on this mission. Fortunately, we accomplished the most important one….. rescuing Sam. The other one was recovering the cross, but Stryker still has that. Portagee saw it around his neck last night. Sometime today I'm sure he'll finish crossing over to St. George's Island. Drax has his lookout post at where Fort George Hill would be in the other world. From there he can watch most of the island. Stryker doesn't have a chance to surprise Drax. In fact it's just the reverse. Drax will be waiting for him. Last night the Nazis were taught about wet gun powder. They won't make that mistake again. I'm sure when they land on St. George's Island they will stop and wait until they're sure their powder is dry. This gives us more time. Alright, Spence we'll update you on our new game plan."

Spence started out, "We're going to split back into two groups again. My group will hustle back up to the North Shore tip again and cross over to Coney Island. Our job will be to wait there and make sure the back door stays closed on Stryker, should he try to escape that way. Jason's group will continue as planned, except for one change. Since we now have the longboat here that team will repair it and row around the south side of the islands and on to St. George's Island. The landing will be at Gate's Bay, where we can hide the boat."

Spence pointed this out on the old pilot's map, because except for the Spinners, no one else knew these locations or names.

Jason now continued: "Once landed, we will move up the east coastline, where we'll still be concealed. From that point on, it gets tricky. First of all we may or may not know if Drax and Stryker have started killing each other. If they have, we can pretty much move at will, no one will be watching the north or east by then. If nothing has happened by then and we chose to move down to the harbour area where Drax has his encampment, the lookout post might also see us." Bubba interrupted: "If that's our only option, then let me and Cooter sneak up the other side of the hill and take it out."

"Great idea," responded Jason.

Then he continued, "That's what we'll do then. Once you guys have taken out the lookout you can join us. After that, it will serve no purpose for you to stay in the lookout. We will lay low and if we determine Drax has the cross then we will wait for the right time to relieve him of it. If it seems he doesn't have it, we'll assume Stryker has it and it will be up to Spence's team to get it back. We have no idea how many pirates are still with Drax. I'm sure he's killed a few off over the years."

Keno spoke up, "Who's teamed up together this time?"

"Good question," replied Spence. "My team will be me, Keno and Michael. Jason's team is the rest of you. Remember you kids, we're not asking you to take anyone out, just be able to defend yourselves. Keno you'll carry a musket. If a gun battle erupts it will be up to Keno and Michael to keep one musket loaded while I'm shooting the other.

Stryker had his SS troopers up at dawn. Indian file they walk into the ocean and swim towards St. George's Island. All of them made it to the island with little difficulty. Stryker knew their powder was wet and it would be pointless to continue. The sun was shining brightly, so he ordered his SS troopers to lay out everything on the beach to dry. Each SS trooper then started cleaning their muskets and made sure the powder was dry. He commanded one SS trooper to move inland about hundred yards to stand watch for any enemy advancements. The SS trooper only had a saber to protect himself. Stryker was a bit confused. He had lost two SS troopers in the last few days to the inferior Pilgrims. What were they up to? The daring rescue of the girl last night in the turbulent weather was totally unexpected. What was driving them? While he was pondering this, he was also admiring the cross which was hung around his neck, unable to discern any connections. He wasn't sure where the pirate's encampment was, so there probably wouldn't be any element of surprise. If he only had proper weapons, like machine guns, Lugar pistols, and grenades, he could make a quick end to the piratical imbeciles. Instead, he was stuck with old muskets and sabers. As he sat there, he finally devised a strategy to defeat the pirates. He would find the right place to set a trap for them. They would be lured into attacking him head-on. When that happened, he would have his men hiding on either side. They would crush Drax like a vise. Like a mad dog protecting its turf, he knew Drax would be overzealous trying to protect his domain and would make a fatal mistake. All he had to do now was to find the perfect place to set the trap. Stryker sent one of his best scouts out to find the perfect ambush spot. Until the scout returned, Stryker would relax and dry out.

The SS trooper moved cautiously along the North Shore trying to stay out of sight and not be detected by a pirate patrol. He had moved about a mile and a half up the coast when he came to a very narrow part of the island. There were two points of interest here for him. First: from here he could see the pirate lookout post, so they also could see the Nazis as they entered the area. Second: there was also a tiny island connected to the south shoreline by a small plank bridge. Drax must use this tiny island somehow. This would be the perfect place to set up an ambush for the pirates. He could place two SS troopers on the tiny island and lure pirates there. The rest of the SS troopers would be hidden in the brush and would open fire on them as they crossed onto the island. The pirates would never know what hit them. With that, he sunk back into the brush and hiked back to the Nazi camp. The SS scout reported to Stryker that he had found the perfect position for the ambush. Stryker was elated. At last he could claim the island for the Fatherland. Tomorrow they would set their trap. But today they would just concentrate on drying out.

Spence, Keno and Michael headed back west and once they cleared the Tucker's Town Point they turned north heading toward the North Shore. While they trekked along the narrow strait of land, Keno and Michael told Spence that there were two large hidden caves in this area. Spence wanted them identified, but the boys could not recall the landscape well enough to find them as everything here was untouched. Keno also pointed out that there was some tiny caves close to the harbour in the jungle area just to the east. Spence took note of this and on they went.

Meanwhile, Jason's team was able to patch up the longboat and shove off for St. George's Island. They caught a good wind and with the help of Bubba and Cooter rowing, it appeared they were going to make good time. Jason made sure they stayed close to the small island to make sure no one saw them coming. Once they were behind St. David's Island they would be safe for a while. The geography of the east end of St. David's was composed of very tall rock cliffs, which totally concealed the small longboat. As they came out of the shadows of the cliffs of St. David's, Jason had them take down the sail, because from this point on they could be seen from St. George's Island if they weren't careful. They then rowed along the east side of Paget Island, where they set ashore until dusk. It was too risky to be seen in the broad daylight on the last stretch of water between Paget Island and St. George's Island.

Once ashore Jason said, "Make sure you stay on the far side of the island. If you go anywhere else they'll be able to see you."

This was especially hard on Portagee and Sam, as they had not seen St. George's since they were in the Triangle and the suspense was killing them. They finally crawled up the hill on their bellies and peeked through the tall grass over the bay at St. George's. To see only a tiny cluster of thatched roof huts was mind-blowing, as they were used to seeing this beautiful small European-style village. Sam got tears in her eyes. She really missed home and wanted to get back.

18

THE BATTLE OF ST. GEORGE'S

As the evening set in, both the Nazis and the Spinners, in their separate teams, began their journey to their planned destination. Jason got his group into the longboat and they shoved off from Paget Island. It was dark enough that they could not be seen. They stayed behind Higg's Island and then rowed through the cut as quickly as possible as this would be the only place someone in St. George's might see them. Once across the cut they pulled into Gates' Bay which was a very small and concealed bay. The Spinners were very familiar with this bay because just up the small hill was where Gates' Fort would have been in their first world. Jason told the team to tie the longboat onto the large tree roots overhanging the rocks on the shore. Now they moved up the eastern shoreline for about a half mile. Once there, they would turn west and try to find a high vantage point where they could watch the encampment and also stay hidden from Drax's lookout.

On the other side of St. Georges' Island, Stryker was having his SS troopers move about a mile along the North Shore. Since it was now dark they couldn't be seen. After a mile's hike along the shoreline they turned south and soon found a tiny clearing to spend the night. Before dawn, Stryker and two of his SS troopers moved across to the tiny island and set the trap for Drax.

Spence's team arrived at the North Shore in time to see Stryker and his SS troopers move inland and out of sight on St. George's Island.

Spence commented, "Guys, this is it. Stryker is going after Drax. So by sometime tomorrow all hell's gonna break loose. I just wonder if he'll be hunting for us next if he survives."

Michael replied, "Yes, but how are we gonna get our cross back"?

"Who knows Michael? The thing is, right now, we're going across to Coney Island and I just can't make up my mind if we should follow Stryker on into St. George's Island."

Keno replied, "At least if we follow, we'll know where the enemy is, and this could be of help. If we stay here, we won't have a clue what's going on, unless they come right back at us."

"OK then, you guys talked me into it. Let's go get wet. Keep that powder dry and the muskets out of the water. Come on."

They waded into the ocean and started swimming towards Coney Island. The team didn't waste any time. They moved across the island and got right back in the water, swimming to St. George's Island. The team waded ashore and immediately checked their muskets and powder to make sure it was dry because Spence did not want what recently happened to the Nazis to happen to him. Spence signaled the boys that he was ready to proceed. They were about an hour behind Stryker, but they would have to be very careful not to catch up to them.

As they were moving along Spence said, "Keep quiet and just follow me. If we loose track of the Nazis we'll stop and spend the night. If we get lucky and find their camp, we'll stop and then we'll shadow them tomorrow. With that, they moved up the North Shore, very cautiously. It was now pitch black out. Spence finally conceded that it would be futile to go on and maybe even dangerous if they accidentally ran into the Nazis. Keno pointed out a small grove of trees that they could move into and not be seen. Spence signaled back a "thumbs up". The team settled in the trees for the night. Tomorrow was another day.

Stryker was up, even before sunrise. He went around kicking and shaking his SS troopers to get them going.

He barked out, "Get your lead butts going, we have some pirates to kill today. This is the day we claim this lost island for the Fatherland."

Within minutes they were on their way to set the trap for Drax. The scout led Stryker down to the opening where the tiny island was, and they stopped just short of the beach waiting for further orders. Stryker pointed out where he wanted the SS troopers to hide in the dense bush. He would signal to them by the waving his saber back and forth, and then they were to open fire on the pirates. He picked his two best marksmen to join him on the island. His plan was to have one of his SS troopers start digging and he would supervise him while his other shooter would hide behind a small hill. He knew Drax would assume that he had found treasure and wouldn't be able to resist the temptation. The spot was ideal, as he knew Drax's pirates would be able to see him from the lookout post.

Stryker was right. Within ten minutes the lookout post had seen the Nazis digging on the island. One of the pirates immediately went running down the hill to inform Drax. It took him about seven minutes to get to the encampment, and he knew not to wake Drax up so he went into Hawkins' hut.

"Mr. Hawkins, Mr. Hawkins, the Nazis are midway in the island." He then shook Hawkins awake.

Hawkins sat up abruptly, "What did you say, mate?"

"The Nazis are already at the small bay."

Hawkins got up and said, "Go get your shipmates ready for some action. I'll go wake Captain Drax."

Hawkins went to Drax's hut, and knocking on the side of the hut Hawkins said, "Captain, it's Hawkins are you awake?"

"Hell no," replied Drax.

"Captain, the Nazis are on the island, they're up to no good."

Drax jumped up out of bed, "Why didn't you say so in the first place," demanded Drax. Hawkins knew to keep his mouth shut.

Drax yelled, "Get the men together."

"Yes Captain, I already have," replied Hawkins.

"Very good," responded Drax as he left the hut to go to the centre of the camp where the men were waiting.

"Hawkins, what are these Nazis up to?" Drax asked.

"There appears to be two to three of them digging for something on the small island," replied Hawkins.

"They must be idiots. There's nothing there. Maybe it's a trap. No matter, let's go pay them a visit they won't forget. Hawkins you take six men and take the trail, then confront them from the land side. You two come with me. We'll come up behind them on the slip point. You other two men go down the north shoreline and come down the hill, just in case there's any surprises."

The pirates broke camp and split up into the three groups to go face the Nazis.

Jason and the rest of the group watched the events in the camp.

Jason said, "O.K., we have to move fast. Bubba and Cooter go to the lookout and take that goon out. He's going to be looking in the other direction watching the action. He'll never hear you coming. Get a quick visual as to what's going on with the pirates, then Bubba you come join us and let us know what's going on. Cooter you stay at the lookout post and continue to watch. If the pirates or Nazis start heading in our direction you hustle your ass down to us. You two move it out quickly. Portagee you and Sam stay with me. We're going to quickly inspect their camp. By the time Bubba gets to us we may know what's going on. If not, then we'll for sure know when Cooter shows up."

They all moved out in their different directions. Both groups were about five minutes away from their targets. Bubba and Cooter were moving up the backside to the lookout post but the spotter had no idea what was going on behind him. Cooter and Bubba both jumped over the railing. It startled the spotter who turned around swinging his musket and hit Bubba in the side with the butt. Bubba fell down and the spotter then turned back the other way, quickly cocking his musket, but before he could fire a round at Cooter, Bubba shots him at close range through the back of his neck. The spotter instantly fell over dead.

Bubba looked over at Cooter and asked, "Aren't you ever going to save my life? I'm always bailing your sorry ass."

Cooter smiled and replied, "Well, cuz you're better than a good luck piece. We better quit jawin' and figure what's going on out there."

They both got up and watched what was going on down below. They could see the pirates surrounding the Nazis, but they didn't see the Nazis in the bush. Bubba headed down the hill to the camp to update Jason.

Meanwhile Jason and the Spinners entered the encampment and start looking around. Down on the harbour shore he saw a sloop, two longboats and one whale boat. All the huts appeared to be only living quarters, except for one which was about four times bigger than the others. They all entered the hut and stared in shock at what they saw.

Sam gasped, "Holy Moses, 'The Lost Treasure of Bermuda' does exist."

The hut had a King's ransom of treasure in it. There were over one hundred chests of treasure in the room. Portagee opened one chest that was full of diamonds, emeralds, rubies and sapphires. His eyes got as big as the jewels.

He then asked, "Jason, do you think they might miss a handful of these babies?"

Jason replied, "It's OK, but don't take too many. I don't want you to sink to the bottom of the bay if we have to go swimming."

Portagee grabbed three small leather pouches in the chest and filled them with jewels, tossing one to Sam, one to Jason, and saved the last for himself.

"Let's go look around the rest of the camp," Jason urged.

They left the treasure hut and looked around some more. Other than food, they only found a large stash of old muskets, sabers, black powder and of course lots of rum. By now Bubba ran into the camp to update Jason with what was happening.

Jason then said, "Bubba! Set a powder fuse to the black powder in the ammunitions hut. Portagee you take a keg of black powder down to the sloop and bust open the end. Then I'll join you to show you how to make a fuse."

Bubba and Portagee got busy with their assignments. Sam stayed with Jason holding the back-up musket. Jason then found an axe for chopping up fire wood. He took it and started chopping holes in the other boats.

When he finished, he turned to Sam and said, "I just want to make sure they can't follow us when we leave."

Sam nodded her approval and returned to the centre of the camp.

Hawkins was cautiously moving his men up the trail towards the Nazis but was still unaware of the ones in the bush. Meanwhile his two other pirates had positioned themselves at the top of the hill behind the Nazis in the bush. The pirates were also unaware that they were there either. Drax and his men were sneaking up behind Stryker from the point. The only thing Drax might do, would be to catch Stryker in a crossfire. He would not attempt to cross the narrow bay.

As Hawkins came into view of the island, about fifty yards away he started to command his men to begin shooting at the Nazis, but before he could do that, the sharpshooter lying down behind Stryker shot first. The bullet hit Hawkins between the eyes. Before he hit the ground the pirates started firing back. The SS troopers in the bush opened fire on the pirates before they could reload. Two of them keeled over. As soon as the other pirates saw the gun smoke from the bush they opened fire on them dropping yet another SS trooper. Stryker never got a chance to make his signal but the battle was underway regardless. As he took aim with his musket, the SS trooper next to him holding the shovel was hit in the back and fell over. He turned around to see where the shot had come from but by then Drax had a lead on him. "Boom!" Stryker was hit in the shoulder. In fact the shot snapped the cross's gold chain and as Stryker fell into the water the cross fell to the ground. The sharpshooter got one more shot off to kill one of the pirates next to Drax before getting shot and killed himself. The remaining Nazis in the bush had seen their leader shot down, but knew they couldn't surrender. Drax would kill them anyway. The remaining three SS troopers reloaded and made one last charge at the pirates in front of them. They were able to kill two of them before they were shot down by the other two groups of pirates who easily caught them in cross-fire. The Nazis were all dead now. The firing stopped and Drax walked back around from the point to check everything out.

Spence, Keno and Michael had been watching the battle as soon as the first shots were fired. Keno had pointed out that the tiny island Stryker was on was what he knew as Bartram Island. Keno was puzzled as to why one of the SS Troopers was digging a hole. They decided to just hide and watch.

By now, Cooter had almost reached the encampment to tell Jason what had happened. Jason saw him running down the hill and went over to meet him.

Panting like mad, Cooter said: "It looks like they killed all the Nazis, including Stryker. Drax and his men took pretty heavy losses also."

Jason turned to the others and said, "They'll be coming this way soon. Everyone except Bubba get back to the longboat. Bubba wait for five minutes and light the fuses. Make sure they are well lit then run for your life over to our longboat. We'll be waiting."

The team ran as quickly as possible towards the longboat without looking back.

Drax reached the site where the Nazis had made their stand, and then began reviewing the losses. Looking down he saw one of the Nazis still alive writhing in pain.

He drew his saber and said, "Die you pig." Then he ran through him with the saber. Keno almost lost it, watching this brutality. He never knew such evil could exist. Drax walked over the small bridge to the island to check out the dead.

He looked around and said, "Where's their Commander Stryker? I shot him dead and he fell in the bay."

There was no sign of Stryker in the water or anywhere else.

Just then Drax looked down and said, "Well look here, Stryker dropped his magical cross in his haste to die."

He bent over to pick it up and said, "This is our ticket out of here. We'll be visiting Shark Hole very soon."

Just as he was broke into a ecstatic smile, "BOOM!".

Then seconds later, "BOOM".

He saw smoke and fire coming from their camp. Two terrible explosions sounded like they had just ripped the eastern end of St. George's Island apart.

He screamed, "Get back to the camp. We're under attack there."

Spence, Keno and Michael were also shocked by the explosions. They were terribly concerned that Drax had the cross and appeared to know how to use it.

Spence said, "I wish we could shoot that cold-blooded killer right now and take back the cross." He knew that was impossible. There were too many pirates with him and they would be risking their lives right now if the pirates knew they were there. The threesome just stayed in their hiding place and watched.

Drax and his pirates ran back to camp and discovered that almost a third of the camp had been destroyed. This was a costly day for the pirates. They lost five men, their ammunition, and who knows what else. Drax ordered one of his men to go back to the lookout to see if anyone else was still in the area or out at sea. He then walked through the camp, hut by hut, to check out the damage for himself. When he walked into the treasure hut he expected the worse but to his surprise it appeared that the treasure was still intact. Drax then went down to inspect the boats. He already knew that the sloop had been blown up, but was dismayed to see the other boats had all been wrecked. The perpetrators had probably arrived by boat. That's why they damaged all the boats so he couldn't follow them.

Drax commanded, "Let's get this place back in shape. Collect up all the dead bodies and we'll burn them. In a few days we'll head out for Shark Hole and try out our magic cross.

Spence knew that Jason's team must have been responsible for the explosions and he was sure they had made good their escape. Knowing that they would have to leave the same way that they sailed to St. George's Island, his team should also head back that way to meet them.

Spence said to Keno and Michael, "This is probably a good time to leave. Drax and his cutthroats are probably not thinking about anything but the mess they found in their camp. But before we go, let's run down to the shore and pick up a few of those weapons. Why leave them for Drax? That will ice his cake for him. He'll even lose his spoils of war." The team then went down and gathered what they could safely carry and still move relatively quickly. Then they were off through the bush back-tracking their way to the western tip of St. George's Island.

The longboat with Jason's team had sailed behind Paget Island and now it would be almost impossible for Drax's lookout to see them. The day was still too young to wait for dark. They would have to sit on the backside of Paget Island until they could make their run for St. David's Island. He didn't want to take the remotest chance that Drax might try to follow in a boat he may have had hidden somewhere. If they waited there, Drax could easily catch up to them. The plan was to take the mast down and row like hell...... just hoping and praying that they would not be spotted. But the bottom line was that Drax probably already knew who blew up his camp any-way.

They made good time running with the wind. and as they came out into the open the mast was lowered and they started pulling hard on the oars for St. David's. Although they didn't know it, they had been spotted by Drax's spotter in the lookout. When they rowed around to the southeast side of the island the mast went up again and off the longboat went. As the longboat sailed around the southeast corner of the island Sam, pointed out the large cave entrance at the base of the cliff. With all the jagged rocks at the base and the waves still crashing on the shoreline, it looked like a treacherous place to land.

Jason commented, "Maybe on a calmer day we could come back and check out the cave."

Portagee added, "Yup, I bet Captain Drax has hidden more treasure in the back of that cave. It looks like not many visitors would venture there."

If the truth were known, Drax had hidden some of his personal treasure there. Pirates tend to have multiple hiding places because they simply don't trust anyone.

As they cleared St. David's, it looked like clear sailing on to Tucker's Point. The crew finally relaxed and began to enjoy the trip. Bubba and Cooter, being old salts, were sound asleep and snoring to beat the band. Jason was handling the tiller and Portagee and Sam, not able to sleep with all the snoring, sat back and enjoyed the ride across the clear turquoise ocean. After about thirty minutes the waves gently

washed them ashore. Bubba, Cooter and Portagee pulled the longboat up off the beach and tied it to an old cedar tree. Until they met up with Spence's team, Jason was unsure what route they would take to go back to Spanish Point and what they should do with the longboat. They hoped to reach Tucker's Point by dusk and hopefully meet up with Spence, Keno and Michael. Then they could compare the day's events and decide what to do next.

Spence and the boys made it back to the main island in very good time. Once they set off for Tucker's Point, Jason asked Keno if he thought he could locate the caves. The terrain was not terribly different, but with no roads and all the dense vegetation it was hard to compare to the other world. If Michael remembered his ancient lore correctly, two boys playing with a cricket ball accidentally lost it in a hole in the ground. When they went in after the ball they discovered Crystal Caves. Keno found the area he thought might be where the entrance was, and they all took their musket butts and began tapping their muskets on the ground. They hoped to find some fissure which would lead to the cave's entrance. After about an hour of tapping around, Spence knew they were running out of time. If they were going to meet Jason's team, they would need to move on soon.

Spence said, "Let's sit down and rest a bit. Then we'll have to get moving."

Michael found a big flat rock to sit on. As he was sitting down his foot slipped on a few loose stones. In a matter os seconds he landed on his butt with his feet sticking up in the air. While he was grimacing in pain, the ground beneath him suddenly collapsed and he sunk into a hole. You could just see his arms, neck, head, ankles and feet. It looked like the rest of his body had disappeared. Keno started laughing and Spence tried his best not to crack up.

Michael started screaming, "Help, get me out of here. I'm sinking. What's worse, something is biting my butt."

Keno and Spence jumped up and grabbed Michael's arms and pulled him up to his feet again.

"Are you alright?" Spence asked.

"Yes, just shook up." replied Michael.

Spence said, "Good, Keno hand me one of those spare torches."

Keno passed a torch to him. Spence lit it and then dropped down on his knees to look into the hole.

Spence said, "Wow, its deep down there. It looks like there could be a small lake way down there. Boy, Michael if you had fallen right through this hole you could have been down there for ages. We don't have a rope so we'll need to come back another day and explore the cave when all this confusion is over."

For a few minutes Keno and Michael felt how it must be to live here without the fear of pirates and the Nazis walking around the island. It was truly a paradise with a new adventure waiting at every turn.

Spence continued, "So much for the fun. We better get moving before Jason and the others worry that something has happened to us."

They started trekking through the jungle again. Michael was following Jason and Keno was bringing up the rear. Keno laughed as Michael was still rubbing his sore tail as they walked along. Michael told him to stifle it or he would give him the same pain as he had. Keno just couldn't stop chuckling.

Drax was sitting on his self-proclaimed throne, gazing at the cross. He couldn't help but notice that the large emerald in the centre of the cross was missing. He thought maybe it had fallen out when he shot Stryker. He decided he would go back pretty soon to look for the missing emerald and Stryker's body. The day for Drax was a mixed bag. Early on he had butchered his perennial enemy, only to have his back side blown off by a foe he never saw.

Just then, one of the spotters came running into camp yelling, "Captain, Captain, I saw a longboat going in the direction of St. David's."

Drax replied, "Could you tell who it was... more Nazis?"

"No sir, I think it was the Pilgrims," the spotter replied.

"Thanks shove off now. Back to your post," Drax snapped. He thought it might have been the Pilgrims, but now he didn't have time to deal with them. That would be for later on. Right now, he wanted to patch things up here and then go visit Shark Hole. He knew there was some mystical power in the cross; all he had to do was figure out how to control it. Drax then yelled out at his men, "Listen here you dirty dogs, I need you two to go collect the muskets from the dead, build a roaring bonfire, and burn the bodies. You three get down to the boats and start patching them up. Don't waste time! Get busy before I run you through". The pirates dispersed quickly, following orders. Drax then got up from his throne and enlisted one of his men to follow him. He was going back to Bartram Island to look for the emerald. By the time he got there his men had a huge pyre burning with all the bodies tossed into the flames. Drax knew this was the best way to prevent disease from starting up on St. George's Island. He turned and asked one of the men who had gathered the bodies, "Did you find the Commander's body?"

"Na Captain," replied the pirate.

"Well, keep looking. I'm positive that we killed him," insisted Drax. Drax then walked over the blood-stained plank to the island to look for the emerald. To Drax's surprise there was no sign of the emerald. He searched every inch of the area where Stryker had been fighting. He wondered if Stryker had removed the emerald and had it on his body. Just to be safe, he told his men that if they found Stryker to be sure to search him for the emerald. Drax finally gave up and returned to the camp. He was thirsty for a bottle of rum. That night they would rest and probably drink far too much rum. Tomorrow was going to be hectic day.

It was late, but the trio found Jason's team on the beach just where the Tucker's Town Point jutted out from the main island. They were all glad to see each other. Nobody had been lost. Jason told Spence and the rest of the trio about the explosions that they had seen and heard. Very excitedly, Portagee told Keno and Michael that they had stumbled upon the "Lost Treasure of Bermuda". They didn't believe him until he pulled out one of the leather bags and dumped the jewels out on the sand. Keno and Michael's eyes got as big as saucers. They were ready to go home and show off the jewels. Spence then related about the battle that they had watched and how all the Nazis were slaughtered……. even Stryker. He also gave them the bad news about the cross, and how Drax had shot it off Stryker and taken it for himself after the battle.

They all knew that it would be hard to recover the cross back from Drax so they might just have to wait a while to get another opportunity.

Jason then said, "Just another day in paradise. We better get some rest. Tomorrow we need to decide how we're going back to Spanish Point and what to do with our longboat."

19

X MARKS THE SPOT

Surprisingly enough, the next day, both the pirates and Pilgrims picked routes that would see their paths cross.The Pilgrims were taking the slow route to move the longboat overland so as to avoid going completely around the island to get back to Spanish Point.

The pirates were going the direct route by water and then a short land trip over to Shark Hole.

Jason and Spence had woken up before sunrise and had formulated the plans for the day.

"Wake up, lazy butts. It's time to get going….. daylight's burning," Spence yelled out.

Everyone started moving around, moaning that it was morning already.

Spence said, "Listen up. We're going to sail the longboat down to St. John's Bay and then move it across land to the Sound."

Everyone started really moaning, not wanting to carry the heavy longboat over the land.

Jason chimed in, "Hey, we can't afford to leave the longboat behind. We don't have enough boats left. So quit whining and get moving."

They all dragged the longboat back out to the water. Everyone climbed in then Cooter and Bubba pushed the boat off and jumped in.

Bubba pointed to Keno and Michael saying, "Guess what boys? It's your turn to row until the wind fills our sail." The boys picked up the oars and started pulling on them. The trip to John Smith's Bay went fairly quickly. They ran the longboat up on the beach, and then everyone helped drag it another thirty feet onto the beach. Keno thought to himself it was going to kill them to drag this boat over the rugged land for over a quarter of a mile. Michael looked over and could see that Sam was visibly upset.

He went over to her, putting his arm around her asking, "What's the matter Sam, you look pretty upset?"

"You're right," she said, "This is where I had to spend the night with the Nazis."

Then she pointed to the rocks where they had spent the night.

"I was scared to death that night, "she said.

Michael hugged her and assured her, "We're here with you now. The Nazis aren't going to bother any one else again."

She said, "You're right. Thanks for caring."

Then she wiped the tears from her eyes and gave Michael a great big hug. Everyone gathered around to the port side of the longboat. They lifted it up and flipped it over "bottoms". Jason then positioned everybody along the length of both sides of the boat. They picked the boat up and trudged along in the direction of the Sound. Sam led the way lifting as much as she could manage. When they arrived at the Sound they would still have to go back to fetch all the supplies they had left behind. It was going to take a long time to move the boat that quarter mile to the Sound. At the best of times, they would move about fifty feet and then have to set the boat down and rest for five to ten minutes.

Back on St. George's Island, Drax picked out his crew to return to Shark Hole to test out the powers of the cross. He had two choices. One was to sail around to what the Spinners knew as Flatt's Inlet, which would be water all the way. His other option was to sail about half the distance to the stretch of land that separates the Sound from the Harbour, and then go over land to reach Shark Hole. His concern was that without a boat he might not be able to get close enough to the entrance of the half submerged cave to activate the power. And as the name aptly warned, he wasn't anxious to swim into Shark Hole, because this was a feeding area for some nasty sharks. Well, needless to say, the more Drax thought about it the more he was convinced to go the long way through Flatt's Inlet. He didn't know it at the time, but this might put him on a head-on collision course with the Pilgrims. Drax picked three of his men as crew members to go with him, the others were going to stay behind to guard the encampment. He wasn't going to have his home blown up again.

The pirates shoved off in their longboat and raised their sail. There was a decent breeze blowing today so the longboat was going to make good time. The exceptional speed came from having only four passengers aboard. After a couple of hours they were out at sea heading along the North Shore. It was at times like this, that Drax and his pirates missed the high seas. They had tried many times to leave the island on various ships but had never found any land. But without proper navigation, except for the sun and stars, they usually got lost or ended back where they started. Drax knew his only way off this island was with the powers of the cross, and that's why he was so much more interested in the cross than the Pilgrims. As they rounded the corner into the inlet he could see that it was still early enough in the day that they would not have to fight the strong current in the inlet. It would be smooth sailing. The longboat entered the Sound. Drax pointed out that Shark Hole was due east on the opposite side of the Sound. The wind in the Sound had dropped to a zephyr so they had to start rowing. It was going to take a long while to get there.

The Pilgrims were about worn out from carrying the longboat across the narrow spit of the island. They could now see the Sound and after one more rest stop they should be there.

As they sat resting Spence pointed across the Sound and said, "Look there's a boat coming across."

Jason pulled out his telescope to and then remarked, "Yes, it's Drax and three of his cutthroats. They're making a beeline for Shark Hole."

Michael jumped up in a panic, "That means they have the Tucker's Cross and it won't take long for him to figure out it will only open the gateway no bigger than a fist. Then he'll come looking for us."

"Hold on, don't get too excited. Right now he doesn't know we're here," Spence replied.

Sam spoke up, "I know we can't get the cross back now, but we need to send a message back home. I know the other night, when we had that big storm, Graham would have been waiting for us, and he's probably wondering what went wrong."

Portagee added, "We need to be there ready to throw a cell phone message through the gateway when it opens."

Jason said, "That's a good idea, but it might be impossible. It looks like Drax is going to row right up to the opening of the cave making it impossible to get around him."

Keno replied, "I could swim under the longboat and with the distraction of the laser and the gateway opening, I could simply toss the cell phone through the gateway, sink back into the water, and swim off."

"That almost sounds good except for the fact that sharks usually feed there," Spence responded.

"I know," Portagee said. "We'll drop all our dried up meat and jerky in the water from just around the corner to draw the sharks away if there are any are close by."

"Now your talkin', you young whippersnapper," Cooter chimed in.

"Alright. It's worth a try, but we better hurry as Drax is almost half way across the Sound", added Jason. Jason fleshed out the plan. Through the dense brush just west of Shark Hole, Portagee and Cooter would slip down to the Sound and distract the sharks in the area with all their dried pork and jerky. Sam would get the phone ready for Keno, so she would go with Keno and Spence and work on it as they walked along. Jason and Bubba were going to stay with the longboat and get it in the water to be ready for the escape. They would also need to dash back to get the rest of the gear that they had left on the beach, and carry it back to the longboat. Keno, Sam and Spence would move around to the east of the cave then Keno would slip down into the water from under the vines and brush that hung down there. Jason and Cooter would be waiting on each side of Shark Hole with their muskets ready to shoot Drax and his men or hungry sharks if anything went wrong. Everyone knew their assignment and took off down the trail that looped around the Sound. While they walked, Sam wrote a little note and wrapped the cell phone in another one of her plastic hair covers. But before she could close it, Portagee told her to add a few jewels and an old Spanish coin that Portagee had found at the camp. Then he also wanted to add a tiny note to let Graham know they had found "The Lost Treasure of Bermuda". She agreed. She now cut off a four inch section of her old cork life preserver, cut it in half and hollowed out a bit. Portagee helped her put the cell phone in between the corks tying it together with one of the straps from her preserver.

Keno took it. Then Spence and he took off at a much faster pace. Sam had to drop the preserver and run flat out to catch up with them. Cooter and Portagee got to their spot first and were waiting for Drax to appear. Portagee heard Cooter munching on something and looked over to see him eating some jerky.

Portagee reached over and slapped his hand saying, "That's shark bait, not Cooter bait. Quit eating that."

Cooter was a bit embarrassed and said, "Sorry I forgot….. you guys didn't feed me breakfast this morning."

The others now reached the other side and went down through the heavy brush to the shore, where Keno could easily slip into the water without being noticed. Now they just had to wait for Drax.

Drax's longboat was now within a couple of hundred yards of the Shark Hole.

He said, "Thar she is mates." Then he moved from the stern to the bow. "Slow down boys. We don't want to enter the cave, just to the opening." Drax blurted out. He still remembered what happened to him the last time he went into a cave. The longboat now passed by where both teams were hiding. This was the signal for Portagee to start putting the dried meat and jerky into the water. Keno slipped down into the water and waited for his opportunity to move towards the cave. Sam handed Keno the cell phone.

Drax now signaled the crew to stop the longboat in the water and hold their position.

He stood up on the edge of the boat and held his arm straight out towards the cave and said, "This is it boys. Let the dark powers of the cave be released!"

The cave started sparking and making sounds. The water in the cave started bubbling. Then with a sudden violent jerk, the green beam shot out of the cross in a triangular form, firing directly into the cave. While all this commotion was going on, Keno started swimming towards the cave, and then as he got within a few feet of the back of the boat he held his breath and dove about six feet under. He then swam straight towards the cave. By now Drax had noticed the green beam was very small and the gateway was also very small. There was no way a man could cross over. Just as Drax was giving up on the gateway, Keno sprang up out of the water just high enough to see the gateway. He threw the cell phone through it. Then, just as quickly, he dropped out of sight.

One of Drax's men yelled out, "What the hell was that? I think a demon came out of the water." Drax dropped the cross down to his side and immediately looked back at his crew. The water calmed down and the cave instantly grew quiet.

"It's a shark you idiot," yelled Drax.

"Like hell it was! Look over there."

The crew member pointed to the shore and saw the legs and feet of Keno scrambling up into the bushes.

"Shoot him," Screamed Drax.

Two of the pirates shot at the bush, but by now the trio was well up the hill under cover of all that dense brush. Meanwhile, Cooter fired a shot back at one of the pirates, hit him in the shoulder and he toppled into the water. He struggled trying to get back into the boat. The water was red with his blood and before they could pull him in, something from below pulled him screaming below the surface of the water.

Drax yelled, "Get out of here, now."

He was mortally afraid of sharks. As they rowed away from the cave he knew something was wrong with the cave, the cross, or both. It then hit him..... the missing emerald must be the problem. Furthermore, someone was waiting for him at the cave. It must be the Pilgrims - they're sneaky. He would have to pay them a visit. Cooter and Portagee also went scrambling up the hill after Cooter fired his musket. They all met on the trail and together hustled back to the longboat. Jason and Bubba were waiting, not knowing what happened. Then they saw Drax's longboat moving much faster leaving the Sound than it had moved when entering. Spence updated the two. They decided it was best to wait until Drax left the Sound as he did not appear to be interested in finding anyone right now.

Graham was sitting in his room playing video games. Ever since his friends had been lost in the Triangle there'd not been much to do. He was worried, especially since during the last storm there was no sign of his friends, not even a glimmer. He was even starting to think that maybe he was crazy. He felt he was trapped in a never-ending nightmare. Graham was bored. He reached over to turn the video game off and just happened to glance down at his cell phone on the floor. The GPS locator light was blinking. Graham started shaking with excitement. He was shaking so uncontrollably he could hardly pick up the phone. Yes, yes it was the Spinner's light blinking. It was Sam's cell phone and naturally it was in the area of Shark Hole. He had to get there right away, but this time he had to make sure that Tattoo Jack's goons didn't follow him. Today, instead of going to the main bus stop in St. George's, he would stick to the North Shore side of town and then go down to the main bus route just outside of the village on Mullet Bay Road. He quietly went out the back of the estate, slipped over the wall and slinked away. If the estate was being watched, they would never know he had left. As he was walking briskly, Graham looked down at his cell phone just to make sure he wasn't dreaming or had lost the signal. Super! It was still blinking. After about fifteen minutes he had turned onto the main road and then just had a very short distance before reaching the bus stop. Not taking any chances, Graham stood behind the bus stop. He couldn't afford to be spotted by the goons. Graham could hear the diesel engine of the approaching bus, so he hurried out to flag it down. The bus driver almost missed seeing him and only stopped at the last second. As Graham got on the bus the driver reprimanded him for not paying attention and he was lucky he caught this bus at all. Graham dropped his zone three ticket into the collection jar and went towards the back of the bus to find a seat. The bus ride seemed to take forever. He must have checked his phone twenty times to make sure the locator was still blinking. Finally he got to the stop closest to Shark Hole and he almost jumped off before the bus stopped. He could tell from the signal that the phone must have floated away from the cave's entrance so he didn't have much time before it floated far out into the Sound. As soon as he got down to the shore he scanned for the phone bobbing in the water or at least a reflection from the silver phone. He kept looking, but couldn't spot it. Its locator was still blinking on his phone. He thought he'd be sick if he got this close and then lost it. What if there was something really important that he needed to know? As he walked along the shoreline staring out at the water, he stepped on something that crunched. Graham lifted his foot up quickly. He thought maybe he had stepped on some poor crab. He looked down and it looked like some old beaten up cork wrapped up in some line. He took another look and then realized it was the cell phone. He picked it up and sat down heavily, hoping nobody would see him. He unwound the cork, being very careful not to damage anything. He knew he would need to show this to the Inspector. Graham pulled apart the two pieces of cork to find the phone inside, wrapped in a plastic hair net like before. He was glad Sam worked part time in the little corner bakery on Water Street. Being around food she was required to wear a hair net. As he pulled open the bag he found the note and hurriedly read it. It read, "Sorry we missed you during the last storm. We were preoccupied and had lost the cross. A pirate named Drax has the cross. We're working on a plan to get it back. It's a long story how we got this note out - will tell you later - we're all fine - don't give up on us - we will make it back. PS, Portagee has something to tell you - bye." Sam "Hey dude, we found the Lost Treasure of Bermuda, see what we sent you, bye dude". As usual Portagee had a way of saying things. Graham looked in the hair net but didn't find anything. He wondered what Portagee could have meant. He then picked up the cork and "Holy Moses", there stuck in the cork, was an emerald and a diamond the size of marbles. He also found the edge of a coin stuck in the cork. WOW! It was a Spanish doubloon dated 1755. Graham sprang to his feet, stuffed his find in his backpack and climbed back up the hill to Harrington Sound Road. As he was about to step clear of the dense foliage, he glanced over and saw Tattoo Jack's truck rumbling down the road. He quickly dropped to the ground and waited for the truck to pass. He could tell from the direction they were going that they must be going into Hamilton to pick up supplies from Gorham's, the big Home Centre. Graham hoped he was right. Once he got onto the road he found it very narrow and serpentine. There was nowhere to hide, so he hoped the bus going back to St. George's would be on time. Thankfully, the bus was right on schedule. While riding back to St. George's on the bus he called Inspector Savage to let him know what had happened and that he was heading back. The Inspector scolded him for not taking him into his confidence and letting him help. Graham had taken a huge risk doing this by himself and could have been hurt. The Inspector would meet his bus at the main bus station, and then they would go to the police station to see what Graham had.

The Inspector was waiting for Graham as he got off the bus, patted him on the back and said, "Good afternoon Graham, let's go."

They walked into the Inspector's office, sat down and Graham pulled out the phone, note, jewels and coin. The Inspector read the note and a tear came to his eye after reading Sam's comments.

Then he looked at the jewels and coin and said, "Graham, these pieces are worth a fortune. This whole mystery is getting bizarre. No one in the world is going to believe this. I just pray to God that they come back soon. From an outsider's point of view, are the kids hiding out, kidnapped or lost at sea? If we show any of this to anyone Graham, they're going to think you're crazy and I'll be fired. Graham let's go see your dad and bring him up to date. Oh! By the way, good job, you're a tough kid. You're doing the right thing. We do know they're alive and well, we're just not sure where they are."

With that they left the Police Station and went over to Graham's father's office. The Inspector spent about an hour with Graham and his father after which they agreed to maintain a 'wait and see' attitude and let the authorities continue on with their investigation. Because his daughter was one of the missing, the Inspector was not part of the investigation. The Inspector decided to do a little research at the St. George's Library on pirates of the seventeenth and eighteenth centuries because now that he had the name of Captain Drax he wanted to see if this pirate ever existed. It didn't take long. In the third book he skimmed through he found him. He had been an ex-British naval officer turned bad. Drax was a ruthless killer who, over a short pirating career, had captured at least a half a dozen ships, presumably with treasure on them. The most frightening statements he read about Captain Drax, were that he was never known to have taken any prisoners. The Inspector decided to keep this little bit of information to himself. The biography of Drax ended abruptly. Apparently he disappeared, never to be heard from again. It was assumed he was caught up in the Great Hurricane of 1780 and was lost at sea. The Inspector went pale when he read this. The Great Hurricane of 1780 had struck Bermuda. He was now sure that this nightmare was real and he feared for the lives of the kids. He left the library and walked down to the docks just to lie low to keep an eye on Tattoo Jack and his goons.

When Jason was finally sure that Drax was well on his way back to St. George's Island, he signaled everyone to pick up their gear and load it into the long-boat. Once everyone was aboard, Keno and Michael shoved the longboat off and jumped aboard. There wasn't enough wind to bother with the sail, so Bubba and Cooter had the honours of rowing. As they rowed, Spence updated everybody as to what had happened at Shark Hole. They had managed to get the cell phone through the gateway and hopefully back to the other world. He also told how Keno narrowly missed being shot and that one of the pirate crew was not so lucky because not only was he shot, he was also attacked and eaten by sharks. The biggest surprise of all was that Drax had figured out that the missing emerald from the cross was the problem why it was not opening up a larger gateway. He was partially correct with his theorizing, but he had not realized he also needed a large lightning storm. This meant that Drax would be going back to his encampment to regroup and then would pay a visit to Spanish Point to lay claim to the missing emerald. Of course, he would stop at nothing. He wouldn't think twice about butchering the entire group to get the emerald. Spence and Jason talked back and forth that they not only needed a plan to protect themselves, but they also needed to recapture the cross. They knew Drax was keen to use the cross, so they could count on him having it in his possession. But what should they try next?

They were getting closer to Flatt's Inlet, so Spence said, "Ease off on the oars, hoist the sail and we'll ride out of the Sound with the tide."

Bubba and Cooter immediately quit rowing. The longboat shot through the inlet like a rubber raft going down a raging river, which was invigorating and relaxing at the same time. By the time they got through the inlet the wind had picked up. They were out of the lee of land now, and they could expect to get fair winds the rest of the way back to the settlement.

The wait in the settlement seemed to last forever. It was disconcerting not to know what was happening with their friends. Georgette and Lynn were standing watch for the afternoon, but they had not seen any activity whatsoever for a couple of days. They always kept an eye on the North Shore, from where they expected the longboat to return. Georgette was gabbing as always. People around her soon wished that she would lose her voice.

Then all of a sudden she hollered, "Look Lynn."

Lynn had tuned her out momentarily.

Georgette then reached over, shook her arm and said, "Lynn, I said look. It looks like our longboat."

Lynn looked through the old telescope. It was them, and they had Sam with them!

She yelled, "You're right." Then they hugged each other and went running to tell Doc and Buford. Buford was asleep, but not for long. The girls barged into the hut shouting.

"O.K., O.K.," Buford said, "I'm getting up. Let's go down to the bay to meet them."

By now Doc had heard the commotion and came running over to see what all the noise was about. Doc said he would stay at the lookout post so the other three could go greet the longboat. The trio made it to the bay well before the boat arrived. The girls stood there waving, while Buford just stood stock still. He was feeling much better, but if he raised his arm his wound might rip open. The longboat hit the beach, the crew climbed out and it was one of those times for lots of hugging and patting on the back. The group unloaded the longboat and headed back up the hill to the settlement. They all congregated around the outdoor cookout area where Jason brought everyone up to speed with what had happened during the past two days. The joy of the reunion quickly evaporated as everybody realized that Drax and his cutthroats would be heading their way soon.

Jason opened the discussion, "I would think Drax would try to attack us from the sea where he could use his boats. However, he knows we have a great observation post here. He could really surprise us with an attack through the jungle, or maybe both ways, but he might not have enough men to do that. Not only do we have to look out for him, but we also need to get the cross back."

Spence pulled out the old Bermuda map and laid it out on the table in front of everyone.

Then he said, "Our biggest problem is that we're too far away from Shark Hole. We need to be able to react to Drax very quickly when he makes a move. What I propose is that we temporarily move over here."

He then pointed on the map to a spot due north of Shark Hole. It was over by Church Bay.

Then he continued, "Here the strip of land is very narrow between the Sound and the Harbour. We'll be close to Shark Hole since we can even see it from Church Bay. Plus Michael and Keno found a cave there that may come in handy for protection. Remember, Drax has a phobia now with caves. We can even hide a small punt just off the beach in the Harbour and only be minutes away from it."

Jason responded, "So far, I like this plan. If we carry it out, we should hide the supplies we leave behind in the caves below. That way they should be safe from Drax. There is just one point you missed, Spence."

"What's that?" replied Spence.

"We still need a small presence here, just in case Drax is monitoring us. We need to make him believe we're still here. If he tries to overrun the settlement then whoever is here will have to flee. If everyone is in agreement with me, who wants to stay and be the caretakers? The Spinners will need to be at Church Bay just in case we get the gateway all the way open. Any volunteers?"

Doc stood up and said, "Well, since I'm a lover and not a fighter, I'll stay."

Georgette then pipped up, "Well in that case I'll stay too."

Everyone else just looked at one another, with lots of smiles and whispering going on.

Doc said, "Oh, shut up, you goofballs. You'd better start getting ready."

The meeting broke up. Everyone had plenty to do now.

20

FINDING THE EMERALD

D rax thought the trip back to St. George's Island was taking forever. He was ready to destroy anything or anyone in his path. As Drax entered, he started barking commands, "You mangy bunch of sea scum, get your useless asses over here".

With that, he sat down on his self-proclaimed throne and waited. When all his men arrived he held up the cross and said, "This is our way home men. When we recover the missing emerald and mount it back on the cross we will be able to get back to the world that we once knew. We will take our treasures and live like kings. We'll be able to plunder any port we choose and kill anyone who gets in our way." Drax then raised his bottle of rum and said, "Drink up mates, for tomorrow the world will be ours." The crew cheered, yelled and chugged down their rum. Drax had no idea that the world had changed so much, and that it would be his doom to return to the real world. Unfortunately, if he did return, the residents of Bermuda might feel his wrath before the authorities could bring him down. Drax would never surrender, so it would be 'kill or be killed'. His plan was to load up three longboats with treasure, then as soon as they recovered the emerald they would open the gateway and row the three longboats directly into the cave, coming out in the other world. The plan was straight forward, but first they had to find the missing emerald.

The Pilgrims had to have it.

With only six crew members still alive after the battle with the Nazis, he knew a direct frontal attack on the Pilgrims was out of the question. He would have to take them by surprise. The pirates decided to use two longboats as well as the whaleboat. The whaleboat was bigger and could carry more treasure. They also loaded one of the long-boats with more treasure. The two boats loaded with treasure would leave St. George's Island and move along the North Shore to Flatt's Inlet. After entering the Sound they would make a sharp turn and row along the shoreline to a small bay the Spinners knew as Tucker's Bay. They would stay there guarding the treasure and wait for Drax's next command. Drax and two of his cutthroats would leave in the other longboat and set ashore somewhere on the main island where they could not be spotted from the Pilgrim's settlement. They would then move across the land and wait for an opportuni-ty to take one or more of the Pilgrims hostage and demand the emerald as ransom. Once Drax had the emerald there was very little chance that the hostage would live. In fact he might still kill all the Pilgrims to make sure the treasure he left behind would be safe. Someday he might come back for more.

The Pilgrims had already loaded up their two longboats and had a good three hour head-start on Drax. They would enter the Sound long before Drax and still stay out of sight. As they pulled into Church's Bay, Jason suggested they land on the south side which was mostly hidden from the rest of the Sound. Here the ground was fairly level and would make an easy place to set up camp. As they started to unload the longboats on the beach, Spence began giving out assignments.

"Buford, since you're still not fully recovered, you'll stand guard, walk around the bay, and keep your eyes on the inlet entrance and Shark Hole."

He then tossed Buford the old ship's telescope and turning to the others he said, "Salty, you and Lynn start getting the fire pit ready to cook in so we can keep warm all night. Be sure to try to keep it out of sight and be sure to burn things that won't smoke much. Spinners, you help me build some makeshift shacks for us to sleep in. I'm sure Jason, Bubba and Cooter are going to do some scouting around between here and Shark Hole to get a feel for the lay of the land".

"That's right," replied Jason. Then he turned and pointed to Bubba and Cooter and said, "Come on cousins, let's go possum hunting."

Cooter jumped totally excited, "Gosh I haven't been possum hunting for years."

Bubba whacked him up the backside of his head and said, "Cooter, what's the matter with you. There ain't no possum here, were just going scouting."

Cooter responded, "Dag nabit, Jason."

Jason smiled and started walking up the hill into the jungle while Bubba and Cooter picked up their muskets and ran after him.

The pirates finally loaded up the boats and set out on their mission. As they left, Drax looked back at his home of over two hundred years. One would assume there would be some fond memories back there, but not with Drax. He cursed the encampment and then went to the bow of the boat. When the pirate boats neared Flatt's Inlet, Drax signaled them to enter the Sound and then on to Tucker's Bay. Drax and his crew went on to the little bay just beyond the inlet entrance. If he went any further along the North Shore he would probably be spotted by the Pilgrims. They landed in the small bay and pulled their longboat up on the beach as far as they could. They then tied the boat up to some trees. Drax had decided to move along the North Shore just out of sight until they were fairly close to the settlement. Once there, they would move south around the settlement and then approach it from the back or west side. Drax felt that the Pilgrims would not be expecting that since the Nazis were no longer on the west end of the islands. It was late in the afternoon by the time Drax was close to the settlement. From his position he could not see any activity. He just thought that maybe he was not in a good place to observe, so he decided to go with his plan and move to the south.

After about forty-five minutes they were in position to approach the settlement. His plan was to try to capture somebody without alerting the whole settlement. They found a spot where they could sneak up without being seen. They waited for ages, but there was no activity. It was getting dark. There were no fires, no candles, no torches burning. The settlement appeared abandoned. Drax became very bold and went from hut to hut but he found nobody. He finally sent one of his men down to the cove to see if there were any boats still there. While he was waiting, he took vengeance out on the Pilgrims by setting fire to their huts.

He then bragged, "Now those damn Pilgrims will know that Captain Drax was been here."

The crewman came back from the cove and reported that there was only a punt on the beach. There was no sign of anyone. Hearing that, Drax cursed and commanded his men to leave. The Pilgrims must have known he was going to take revenge for what they did to his camp and had fled for their lives. So they just smashed down the front gate and left.

Doc and Georgette hadn't heard a thing. Just before dusk they had moved down to the caves for the night, knowing they would be safe from the pirates there. The next morning, Doc and Georgette went back to the settlement to find it in ruins. There was no point in staying at the settlement any longer but the question was, how could they contact their friends to warn them without running into Drax on their way? Doc knew the North Shore sea route was open, however, they might be ambushed at Flatt's Inlet, or even worse, lead the pirates to their friends at Church Bay. Georgette questioned if they should even try to warn the group. After all, they already knew Drax would be looking for them. They just didn't know when. Both decided to cross the central part of the island, but stayed on the south side and then on to the South Shore. Taking the long way around would surely let them miss Drax and his cutthroats. They packed what could be found and left the burned out settlement.

Drax and his men spent the night in the middle of the island. He was at a loss as to where the Pilgrims might be. They just had to keep searching. He was sure they would be somewhere on the main island but probably not the East or West End. This morning he was going back to Tucker's Bay to get two more of his men. They had been left to watch the treasure. That ought to be enough.

All was well in the morning at Church Bay. The shacks had been finished the night before, and Portagee, Michael and Keno had caught over ten Spiny Lobsters in the Sound. Salty, Sam and Lynn had boiled them in Salty's two hundred year old pot over a large camp fire. The feast that night had been perfect, and almost everyone had forgotten their problems.........at least for the night.

Today Jason and Spence desperately wanted to devise a plan to deal with Drax without getting anyone in the group hurt or killed. They were positive that Drax would be looking for them to recover the emerald or to take a captive as ransom for the emerald. At the same time, they both knew Drax possessed the cross, which meant they needed a plan to alleviate him of it. So they had to stay away from Drax yet at the same time they had to be close enough to him to recover the cross. Talk about contradictory ideas. They would have to be the aggressor with a 'hit and run' tactic or set a trap in the hopes that he would fall for it.

Jason explained, "Drax will be looking for the camp. We should visit the cave you and the Spinners found to see if we can make a temporary home there. I think this site will end up being too easy to find."

Spence agreed. He then went to instruct Bubba, Keno and Sam to go to the cave and see if they could inhabit it for a short period of time. The trio picked up some torches, rope, two picks and a shovel, then headed for the area Keno and Sam knew as Crystal Caves. Jason and Spence brought the rest of the camp together to fill them in on the plans. They were told to hide the longboats in the bush and then start preparing to move out in the morning to go to the caves. Buford, Salty, and Lynn would be the ones to get the camp ready, while Michael, Cooter and Portagee would help Spence and Jason start rigging booby traps around the area. Michael would go with Jason and Portagee would go with Spence. Cooter was an old backwoodsman at home and would do just fine on his own. Everyone headed out in three different directions with ropes, hatchets and anything else they thought they could use. It was agreed that the traps would be placed along the trails only, and after all of this was over they would go back and destroy any remaining traps. Cooter liked the snares, rigging up more than twenty in just a few hours. Cooter had also crushed old glass bottles and laid the small razor sharp pieces on the dirt trails, dusting them over with dirt. He thought that most of the pirates might be barefooted. In areas where the trails were dark from heavy foliage and tree overhangs, he tied small vines from tree to tree and made tripwires out of them. Then where the pirates would fall, he placed small sharpened spikes sticking out of the ground. These were guaranteed to inflict pain wherever they stuck. The idea was to inflict pain on the pirates, maybe 'cause some dissention in their ranks and maybe they might turn on each other. With that, Cooter scouted around a little more to see if any pirates were in the area and then decided to head back to camp. He was getting hungry. The other groups were not so creative; they basically kept to the good old snare tactics. They then also returned to camp.

Keno had lead his group back to the opening that Portagee had accidentally opened. Sam couldn't help but laugh when she saw the hole, as it reminded her of the story the others had come back and told. Bubba started chiseling away at the opening making it much larger, and as luck was on their side they had actually broken through on a ledge with a natural walkway down to a lower level of the cave. It looked like the water, over thousands of years, had etched a natural bumpy groove in the cave floor which resembled irregular steps going down the slow sloping incline. The trio lit up their torches and went down into the cave where there were beautiful stalactites and sta-lagmites all over the cave. Bubba had never seen anything so amazing as this in his life. At the bottom of the cave there were the most breathtaking small lakes that looked like they were hundreds of feet deep. There was no way any of the pirates would ever have the courage to enter this cave. They soon found the perfect place that was large enough for them to make a small encampment. With the high ceilings it would be safe to have fires in the cave as the smoke would rise and find its way out through the entrance.

While Sam was busy cleaning up the area, to call it home, and making a small fire pit, Keno and Bubba needed to see if they could find another way out. Although Drax and his cutthroats would not enter the cave they might still shoot their muskets through the entrance of the cave or just wait outside and ambush them. While they were inching along a narrow ledge, Bubba's foot slipped on the damp, slick ledge and the next thing everyone heard was a huge splash, which echoed all over the cave.

Sam came running just to hear Bubba yell, "Holy crap! It's cold down here; get me out of here before I turn into an iceberg."

Keno couldn't help but laugh a little once he knew Bubba was OK. He then said, "You've never even seen an iceberg."

He and Sam then reached over to give Bubba an arm and pulled him out of the cold water. With that, the two guys went back to their searching and Sam went back to her organizing.

A few hundred yards into the cave Keno saw the light rays shining through the wall of the cave.

Bubba pulled out the pick and said, "Let me at it. This reminds me of when Buford and I broke out of the Yankee prison camp back in the war."

In about an hour they had a hole chopped through the side, large enough for a person to crawl through. This was great. The escape exit opened up in the jungle area east of the entrance. Drax would never find this opening into the cave. After wrapping up everything the trio headed back to camp.

Late that afternoon everyone had returned to camp. Dinner was waiting, so while everyone sat around the pit fire eating, each group described what they had accomplished that day.

As usual Jason led the meeting and he began by saying, "Tomorrow we need to break camp and move on to Crystal Cave to setup our camp there. With the back door over two hundred yards away from the entrance we should be safe and can escape if need be. When we get there we need to setup some tin can and bottle trip lines, so if the pirates try to sneak up on us at night we will know. Also during the day one person must stand on guard detail outside the entrance 100 percent of the time. Spence will work up a schedule for everyone to take part in the guard duty. Tonight, while it's still fresh in everyone's minds, we need to make a diagram, as detailed as possible, of a map to show where all the booby traps are located. Once we do that, everyone needs their own copy of the map to carry with them. I don't want to find one of you swinging upside down after being caught in a snare trap somewhere."

Bubba piped up by saying, "I'm sure Cooter will be the first one caught and in his own trap too." Cooter responded, "If you weren't kin I just might hang you by your big fat toes right now, Bubba."

The group all laughed, then Jason continued, "OK guys and girls, let's keep this a little serious. We also have not heard a thing from Doc or Georgette. I'm sure by now Drax has been to the settlement so let's all pray that they both escaped unharmed. Tomorrow we need to send out a scouting party, not only to be on the lookout for Drax and his cutthroats, but also for Doc and Georgette. We don't want them to run into Drax or any of our booby traps. I think we all need to get a good night's rest and be ready for a busy day tomorrow. I will give everyone their assignments in the morning. Any questions?"

No one had any questions. Part of the group went to their makeshift huts to go to bed and the Spinners stayed up by the fire to talk. Bubba and Buford also stayed with them.

It was pitch black out that night, in spite of the full moon.

The ghostly clouds floated through the sky, shadowing out the moon, until it seemed like an eerie glow. Buford could tell the Spinners seemed a little nervous this night.

He then winked at Bubba and said, "On nights like this, back home in Louisiana, sometimes the creatures of the night come out.... did you kids know that?"

The Spinners all looked at each other and shook their heads - no.

Portagee asked, "What do you mean Buford?"

Buford responded, "You all know, growing up back in the swamps, when we were in bed supposed to be asleep, we could hear them."

"Hear what?" whined Sam.

Buford replied, "The Putty Pickers."

"The, what?" Michael said.

"You heard me, the Putty Pickers," Buford raised his voice. "These creatures of the night are bigger than a rabid wolf, with long claws about eight inches long and a sharp hooked beak. They also have Spanish moss hanging all over them from where they hide up in the trees during the day. The Putty Pickers use these long razor sharp claws to pick out the putty in the windows of children's rooms. After all, adults are too big for them to carry off into the swamps to devour. So, on nights like this, you might hear them scratching away at the putty in your windows and sooner or later your window falls to the floor and shatters into a thousand pieces. Then you hear this terrible sound of these claws screeching across the floor heading toward your bed. Then as they climb up onto your bed their claws slice through the sheets and rip them to shreds. You can't move, you're terrified with fear. Then all of a sudden, the Putty Picker leaps at your neck with its deadly claws and, and........"

"And what?" yelled Portagee.

"I don't know, I woke up," laughed Buford.

"Come on Bubba let's get to bed, I don't want to be out here if the Putty Pickers show up."

They both got up and headed for their hut. The Spinners looked at each other, then looked into the darkness of the night and quickly got up and walked as fast as they could to their huts.

21

REFUGE IN CRYSTAL CAVES

E arly the next morning Bubba, Cooter and Portagee left the camp and headed south to watch out for the pirates, but mostly to watch for Doc and Georgette. The rest of the group began tearing down the camp and preparing to move it to the cave.

Doc and Georgette were on the move at sunup. They had taken the long way around making sure to try to avoid Drax, wherever he was. They were now moving north towards Church Bay, keeping on the trails making sure they would not get lost. Doc was in the lead and as luck would have it "swish", he was scooped up and dangling by one foot.

Georgette let out a shriek, "Doc, Doc, are you alright?"

Doc responded, "Yes can't you tell, I'm just hanging around. Want to join me?"

Georgette was so scared she was jumping around and then, "swish", she too was bobbing around like a top.

Doc then said, "This might be funny if I knew we weren't in a trap set by Drax."

Georgette stammered out, "What can we do?"

Doc then said, "Whatever you do don't scream, we don't know who's in the area. You might try to pull yourself up and try to loosen the vine."

"Sure thing, Doc, and then I can drop five feet to the ground and land on my head," Georgette snapped back.

Doc then said, "No problem, I'm a doctor I would help you. Oh, maybe not, I forgot I'm up here with you too."

"Your very comforting Doc," Georgette sighed.

"Well we'll just hang around for awhile and wait for some help," replied Doc.

The trio had been on a due south course for about an hour, staying off the trails.

Bubba raised his hand to signal to stop, and then he whispered, "Did you hear that?"

Cooter and Portagee shook their heads that they had heard nothing. Then there it was again, crackling in the trees, now they all heard it. Bubba signaled to move forward. They did, but very slowly and quietly.

Just then Doc heard someone coming through the bush, he whispered, "Hey is that you guys?" He heard back, "Yes, it's us you whining Pilgrim."

Then out of the bush stepped two pirates. One looked to the other and said, "Well look here. Drax said we would find some stupid bloody Pilgrims, and look here we did. Check their bags for the emerald."

The other pirate looked through their belongings as the other one aimed his musket at Doc.

"Nothing here, but junk," said the one pirate.

The other one said, "Drax told us no prisoners, so let's just kill them and get going."

He then cocked back the firing hammer on his musket and started to squeeze the trigger. Something came like a lightening bolt from the bush. The pirate heard a "thud", he looked down and saw a knife stuck in his chest, and then fell over dead. The other pirate dropped his musket and ran for his life.

Bubba, Cooter and Portagee came running out of the bush. Portagee lifted Georgette's shoulders up while Bubba did the same for Doc. Cooter bent over the dead pirate and pulled the knife out of his chest, wiped the blood off of his knife on the pirates shirt. He then turned to cut the vine that was holding Georgette up and did the same for Doc.

Bubba then said, "How long you guys been hanging around?"

"Very funning," said Doc. "Can we get the hell out of here?"

Portagee then said, "What about the other pirate, .. he got away?"

Cooter replied, "He's half way back to China by now, we'll never catch him. You can bet one thing now; Drax will be heading this way soon. Let's reset these snares and get out of here. Georgette, are you alright? Bubba, pick up those two muskets, I'm sure they'll come in handy." He nodded his head yes and everyone headed back to the camp. Bubba decided to stay behind a couple of hundred yards to make sure no one was following them. By the time they made it back to the camp, it was deserted.

"That's great, now how do we find the cave?"

"No problem," said Portagee, "I know the way, just follow me."

They left Church Bay and headed for Crystal Cave.

It took two hours, but the lone pirate made it back to Tucker's Bay. The lone pirate stumbled into the camp and all but collapsed at the feet of Drax.

Drax reached over, grabbed the pirate by his hair, jerked his head up and demanded, "Where's your ship mate you bloody idiot?"

The pirate responded in pain, "He's dead Captain, the Pilgrims killed him."

"What!" screamed Drax. "Those puny Pilgrims killed him. Were you sleeping?"

"No sir, we found two of the Pilgrims caught up in a snare. It must have been theirs or one the Nazis had set. We searched them for the emerald but they did not have it. Then we started to shoot them, when, out of the bush, a knife was thrown and hit my mate in the heart."

Drax asked, "Why didn't you shoot them?"

The pirate, fearing for his life thought for a minute, then responded, "Four of those cowardly Pilgrims then jumped out of the bush and tried to kill me. I had to fight for my life and finally got away into the jungle."

"So you lost your musket in the fight to?" asked Drax.

"I Captain, the musket snapped in two when I clubbed one of the Pilgrims over the head with it," replied the pirate.

Drax in a fit of fury picked up his bottle of rum and struck the side of the pirates face with it, causing the bottle to shatter to pieces upon contact.

Drax then screamed, "You bloody liar, I should run you through right now and be done with you. You're a lucky scum bucket, I need you right now."

"Oh! Thank you. Oh! Thank you," the pirate cried as he kissed the feet of Drax.

Drax kicked him in his head and walked off.

Portagee led the group across the narrow land mass between the Harbor and the Sound and finally they came to the clearing entrance where the cave was. Spence was on watch. He had already seen them coming and alerted the others. Everyone came out to greet the late arrivals. Doc and Georgette each took turns updating everyone how the pirates had set fire to the Spanish Point area settlement and how they were snagged in Cooter's snares. Then Portagee told of how pirates were ready to shoot Doc and Georgette, when Cooter threw his knife in the chest of one of the pirates, the other pirate ran for his life.

After listening to the story the group moved down into the cave, leaving Bubba to guard the entrance of the cave. The area of the cave they had selected to call home for a while was very comfortable and spacious for a cave. Salty already had a small fire going to give some light along with the torches propped up in the rocks. The early arrivals had carried a very adequate supply of firewood down, enough to last several days. Spence then showed the new arrivals the escape route from which to exit, at the back of the cave, should they need to. Doc suggested they hang some bottles and cans across the back entrance, covered up by a little brush, to offer an early warning system should the pirates try a sneak attack. Spence agreed that was a good idea and it would be done before dark.

Once back to what Sam called the Great Room, Jason told the others, "Since we've not had an encounter with the pirates, they know roughly where we are, so we will have to be very careful and keep to the buddy system. No one goes out anywhere on their own, you always have to have someone with you at all times. Tomorrow we'll send out three groups to scout around for the pirates, remember, we only want to get the cross back. I'm one hundred percent positive that Drax will keep the cross on him. If you run into any pirates without Drax there's no point in making any contact. You can follow them for a short distance to see where they're going, plus you might overhear a conversation they're having. We'll pair up as follows; I will go out with Keno, Spence will go out with Bubba, and Cooter will go out with Michael and Portagee. The rest of you will stay here and keep an eye out on the cave. With that everyone broke up in their little groups for the evening. Bubba did ask the Spinners if they wanted to stay up and hear any stories. They assured him that that was not necessary and they were slightly tired. Bubba smiled and walked off.

22

DRAX CAPTURES THE EMERALD

Drax was still burning with anger. They slaughtered the Nazis, a hard core military unit, then got whipped and sent away like dogs with their tail between their legs by the Pilgrims. He now knew roughly where the Pilgrims were hiding, so he decided on a surprise attack tactic. He would send two pirates back the same way as the others were today and they would try to find them moving up from the south. This is where the Pilgrims would be expecting them. He, however, with three pirates, would swing in from the north and hope to surprise them. One pirate would stay behind and protect the treasure, just in case of a surprise attack from the Pilgrims. With his plan in place to find the emerald, Drax laid down by the fire with a bottle of rum and soon passed out.

The next morning everyone slept in a little late because of the darkness of the cave. The scouting groups were anxious to get going so they elected not to have Salty cook up something. They had some fruit and jerky and moved out very quickly. Jason and Keno went south towards Shark Hole, Spence and Bubba went west, back towards Church Bay and Cooter, Michael and Portagee went towards North shore. The North Shore scouting team was really not expected to run into anyone, that's why they had two Spinners in their group. Jason and Keno were going to Shark Hole to stake it out. They would hide just to the north of it, on a hillside, to see who might show up. Spence and

Bubba, after going to Church Bay, would use their hand written maps and check out all of the traps to see if they had caught any two legged game in them.

Drax's groups had also gotten off to a late start that morning because they all had hangovers from drinking too much the previous night. He believed that the best way to get over a hangover was to have some more of the snake that bit you the night before, so he popped open another bottle of rum and after a few gulps he was ready to go. The morning was a bit overcast, but outside of that it was a nice day for a hike so the two groups set off in different directions with plans to meet late in the afternoon at Shark Hole. Drax and his men tried to stay as close to the shoreline as possible on the north shore of the Sound without being seen. The other two did the same on the west and south shores of the Sound.

Jason and Keno were now in position and watching Shark Hole from under a nice shade tree with a breeze. Spence and Bubba had made it to the Church Bay camp and saw no signs of anyone else having visited the camp. They then headed back towards the traps to see if any of them had been set off. Cooter and his group had no particular destination, except go towards the North Shore. When they reached the North Shore, Cooter wanted to go check out Coney Island from the shoreline without going over to the island. Michael and Portagee said they would wait for him there on the rocks over-looking the North Shore. He said that was OK and that they must stay there to wait for him to come back. He then went over the hill and was out of sight. Michael and Portagee just sat there talking about their adventures and the fact that no one would ever believe their story, if the ever made it back to the other world. Michael surprised Portagee with the comment that he was not sure if he even wanted to go back, saying that he really liked it here. They continued to relax and threw a few rocks at the ocean. Portagee then commented that he wished he could catch up with Captain Drax and make that dirty pirate walk the plank. At that moment both Michael and Portagee felt a sharp object sticking in the back of their necks.

"Well my little cabin boys, we'll see who's going to walk the plank," responded Drax. "Don't move you little sea scuppers, unless you want our sabers through your skinny little necks."

Michael and Portagee thought they were about to die.

"OK, OK," replied Michael. What do you want?"

"Stand up and turn around," yelled Drax.

They did as they were told. Michael was shocked; this was the ugliest, meanest and most dirty person he had ever seen.

"Empty out those pockets boys before I run you through," Drax demanded.

The boys did. Michael knew what he wanted and tried to hide the emerald between his fingers, but what little sun there was, cast a ray on the emerald causing it to sparkle radiantly.

Drax immediately saw this, and then hit Michael with a strong backhand knocking him off his feet. Towering over Michael he stomped his dirty boot down on Michael's chest, then stuck his saber in his throat. "Boy you have one second to hand me that emerald or I will run this saber through your throat."

Portagee yelled, "Michael, give it to him."

Drax replied, "Your little Portuguese friend is right."

Michael then raised his hand up and gave Drax the emerald.

Drax then lifted up his boot and pulled back the saber and said, "Get up, we need to get going."

Michael said, "You don't need us now, you have the emerald."

Drax laughed, "Yes and I want to make sure we keep it too, you two runts will be our safe passage back to our world, now let's get going."

Both boys were grabbed by their necks and shoved along heading back towards Tuckers Bay along North Shore. Michael as he was walking dropped his Spinners keychain and pressed it into the dirt with his foot in hopes that someone would find it. As Portagee walked by the keychain without thinking he quickly picked it up and clipped it on his belt loop. Drax was already carefully fitting the emerald back into the cross.

About fifteen minutes later Cooter came back over the hill yelling, "No sign of any pirates over there." He then looked around and yelled, "Boys where the Sam hill are you? Come on out."

No one responded. Cooter was now worried, he looked over the rocks to make sure they hadn't fallen into the ocean. He then started looking around the area for tracks; however it was too rocky to find any. Then out of the corner of his eye he saw a unique print on the ground, he walked over to it and found the imprint of the Spinner keychain. Cooter now knew the boys were in trouble, he wanted to follow them, but he knew he better go get help. Cooter set out on a dead run back for the cave.

While he was on his way back, Jason and Keno had been watching two pirates at Shark Hole. They seemed to be waiting for someone and appeared to be very nervous. Finally Cooter made it back to the cave and told Buford what had happened. Buford told Cooter he better find Spence and Jason as quickly as possible. He headed straight for Shark Hole, thinking it might be easier to find someone there. Sure enough, he found Jason and Keno and told them what had happened.

Jason responded, "We need to get going, but what should we do about these two cutthroats? They seem to be waiting, but I don't think Drax will show up now that he has Michael and Portagee."

Cooter said, "Let me sneak down there and they will never know what hit them."

Jason responded, "We're not killers, but we will defend ourselves."

Just then out of the bush, "Bang" ...then a couple of seconds later, "Bang". The two pirates fell over the rock ledge into the Sound. Their bodies floated lifelessly in the water. By tomorrow they would either be carried out to sea or a dinner for the sharks. Jason and the others dropped flat on the ground not knowing what was going on. Jason finally looked up and pointed over to the dense bush where musket smoke was floating through the air. For a split second Keno thought he saw an eye blinking through the bush and then it was gone.

Jason whispered, "Backup and crawl down the hillside as quietly as possible."

Once out of sight and out of musket fire range they stood up and Cooter asked, "What the hell just happened back there?"

Jason replied, "I know it wasn't Spence or Bubba and I'm sure Drax is going another direction now, so there must be someone else here that we have not accounted for."

Keno said, "But who?"

Jason replied, "I don't know, but we're not staying around here any longer to find out. I don't like his greeting."

With that they made their way back toward the cave, but not in a direct approach, if they were being followed they wanted to make it hard to be tracked. Cooter lagged behind a ways, and off to their left, just to make sure they weren't being followed. Two thirds of the way back they ran into Spence and Bubba and told them what had happened, as they moved together in the direction of the cave. Upon their arrival Jason had Buford go get the others in the cave and he then told them what happened. Now there was someone else in the area that appeared not to have a problem killing people. Buford and Bubba stayed on guard while the others went below so Jason could issue everyone some type of weapon to protect themselves.

Michael and Portagee were being shoved by the pirates, about every tenth step they took. Drax was paying very little attention as he was mesmerized by the cross. It was now complete and he had the power to return home to be one of the most powerful pirates in the high seas. He had been waiting for over two hundred years for this opportunity and was not going to let it slip through his hands. No one was going to get in his way, no one.

He finally looked up at the Spinners and said, "Boys, what be your names?"

Michael responded first, "It's Michael, sir."

"And you boy?" Drax Demanded.

Portagee was very cautious because of his nationality, knowing that Drax probably hated the Spanish and Portuguese, so he used his real name.

"My name is Roderick." It was a very good English name.

Drax responded, "Very good lads, make sure you don't cross me and you may live to tell about it."

As they walked along towards Tucker's Bay, Drax was thinking about when he would next be able to use the cross. He already figured that if he wanted the full power of the cross like the night it brought him here, there would have to be a heavy lightening and thunder storm. Now he would have to keep the Pilgrims at bay until a storm developed. They returned to the camp just before dark and discovered his other two men had not returned. Surely they were still not waiting for him to show up. He knew they were stupid, but not that stupid. Drax suspected that they probably would not be back, not because they were lost, but because they were dead. He had now lost more men in the last few days than he had in the last hundred and fifty years. There were only four of them left. They would have to be very careful, but the good news from this is that the share of the treasure was now bigger for each of them. He would have to sleep on it - as how to protect the cross. He didn't want to be very far away from Shark Hole in case of a storm. Any rate, a bottle of rum and a little sleep might help. He then barked at his men to tie Michael and Portagee up to a tree for the night, and then they threw blankets over them.

That night the Pilgrims sat around the fire trying to decide what course of action to take. They knew that Drax had Michael, which meant that he had probably already found the emerald. He must also know by now that he needs the aid of a storm to open the gateway large enough to pass through. He appears not to understand that the world had changed over the last two hundred years, or why would he want to go back. At this point Drax would now probably try to avoid us, in fear of losing the cross. Also, he would hold Michael and Portagee as hostages to protect the cross from being stolen from him. One bit of good news is we probably now outnumber the pirates, but with the boys being hostages that may not be of any help. Plus, who is this mystery shooter? Would he have also shot us if he had seen us? The group decided to be safe and cautious. They did not want to do anything to put the lives of Michael and Portagee in jeopardy. Two members of the group would keep watch on Shark Hole for any activity. If there was any, then one of the watchers would run back and tell the others, while the other would stay and watch. Also, starting tomorrow, a scouting party of three would head towards North Shore to try to pick up the trail of the pirates and try to find where they are holding the boys.

Salty and Lynn were up early cooking codfish for breakfast hence there was no need for wake up's this morning. The smell of the fresh fish being fried, floated throughout the cave. Everyone was up and ready to eat.

Salty finally yelled, "Come and get it while it's hot off the skillet."

Buford, Bubba and Cooter were first in line. However, they did let Sam and Georgette move to the front, but anyone else went to the back of the line. After breakfast Jason and Spence made the assignments for the day. Buford and Keno drew the detail to keep an eye on Shark Hole; Keno, because of his youth, would be the runner if the need arose, in order to get back to the cave quickly. Spence, Bubba and Cooter were going to head to the North Shore to try tracking the pirates.

Buford and Keno were first to head out but because of the surprise in the bush the day before, they decided to go in the direction of the Sound and follow the shoreline to Shark Hole. On the way, they went down to Church Bay to check on the longboats - they were still hidden and not disturbed. They then turned south and stayed on the shoreline all the way to Shark Hole. Instead of going up on the hillside they stayed close to the shoreline, as this way they could watch Shark Hole and not have to worry about a sniper in the bush.

Spence was content to follow Bubba and Cooter because he knew they were excellent trackers from the years they had spent in the swamps of Louisiana. It was much easier to track in the muddy swamps than in the rocky North Shore area. The rocks of North shore were not conducive for tracking. Once on the North Shore the trio headed west, moving towards the Flatts area, even without tracks they were sure Drax would stay close to the Sound waiting for a thunder and lightening storm.

Drax must have had a good night's sleep because when he woke up in the morning he had a great idea to protect the treasure and the cross. He quickly got up and started yelling at his men to wake up.

"Get your bloody butts up, we've got work to do and fast."

He started kicking the sleeping pirates to get them up and moving. Michael and Portagee were already awake; in fact they had slept very little during the night. Drax commanded his men to break camp as soon as possible and load up the longboats with their gear. Although his men grumbled about not getting any breakfast, they still followed orders, without question. About thirty minutes later the longboats were loaded and the pirates were ready to shove off. The three longboats rowed out towards the middle of the Sound. Michael and Portagee were forced to row, and for security reasons they were separated into two different longboats. Moving out towards the centre of the Sound, Drax pointed to where he wanted them to go. It was a tiny island out in the middle of the Sound, which would be easy to defend and no one would be able to sneak up on Drax without him knowing about it.

Portagee looked to the island where Drax was pointing; he knew it as Crow Island. From Crow Island the pirates would be almost fifty percent closer to Shark Hole and have good vision of the cave entrance. The longboats landed on Crow Island, they

were quickly unloaded and the mini encampment was setup in a couple of hours. Drax knew this was a big gamble. In a way he had trapped himself on the island, but he needed a way to protect the treasure and the cross. He was now able to watch the entire island, with two men rotating and a third pirate who would rest when not on duty. Michael and Portagee would now find themselves tied up most of the time. Drax was paranoid and it was beginning to wear on him, as if he could be any worse.

Cooter finally found some tracks.

"Look," he said, "It's definitely the boy's. See the funny squiggles and circles in the prints?" Spence and Bubba agreed that there were only four sets of shoes on the island that leave these funny prints. Cooter then saw the Spinners keychain imprint in the dirt, he knew for certain they were on the right trail now. Cooter took the lead and the other two followed. The tracks took them more inland. Soon the tracks lead them to a hog trail, so they took the trail that lead west. Since the pirates went on a trail they were more interested in making speed, not caring if they were being followed.

Spence noted, "With Michael and Portagee being held as hostages, Drax must not be very worried that we might try to do him in."

Bubba responded, "Yeh, but Drax has forgotten he butchered our crew years ago, but I haven't forgotten."

Spence chimed in, "Bubba that was almost one hundred fifty years ago, let it go. I don't want revenge clouding your head."

"Well I'll be darned, a Yankee's talking sense to me, times a changing, your right," responded Bubba.

Cooter then said, "Guys, daylight is burning. Can we stop the small talk and git going?"

The trio went on down the trail hoping it would lead them to Drax's camp. After about two hours of following the tracks down the trail, the tracks finally left the trail and ended up at Tucker's Bay. Cooter could see well ahead of arriving at the bay that no one was there any longer. They walked down on the beach looking for clues for Drax's whereabouts. The fire was still smoldering from last night, it had not been cooked that morning, but Cooter figured that they left in a hurry early. But why? Spence walked down to the shore where the three boats had been, noticing that based on the tracks in the sand, that the boys were put into two different boats. They must have needed them to row. Cooter then pointed out that the deep grooves in the sand meant that the boats had heavy loads in them. What could they be hauling?

Bubba then said, "Holy cow, these cutthroats have the treasure with them and they're going to take it back to the other world with them."

Spence said, "Where in the hell did they go? With these heavy boats they would- n't want to go far. Their only choice would be to go to Shark Hole or just get closer."

Cooter added, "Look, there's no place for them to hide at Shark Hole and if they tried Buford and Keno will see them."

Spence told the other two it was time to split up to see if they could find where Drax had gone. It was safe to assume that they were still in the Sound somewhere. There would be no tracks to follow now and without a boat they would have to circle the Sound and hope to get a visual sighting of them. It was decided that Bubba would cir- cle around the Sound on the west and south side; therefore, he would get to Shark Hole quicker that the other two. Spence and Cooter would go back the same direction they had come from, except that this time they would stay to the shoreline. With that, Bubba swam across the Flatts Inlet and then went on down the western shoreline, while Cooter and Spence headed out along the north shoreline. This shoreline has many small coves and bays so it was going to take them much longer to get back, but they did not want to take any chances on missing Drax. Bubba worked his way around the Sound passing Devil's Hole and on to Shark Hole, with no sign or trace of Drax. Keno spotted Bubba and signaled to him by whistlin'. Bubba went down the hillside through the dense brush and down to the shoreline. He then told Buford and Keno how they had found where Drax had been camped on the beach at Tucker's Bay, but no sign of Drax. Spence and Cooter had the same luck as Bubba - it was like Drax and his boats had vanished into thin air. When they got to Church Bay, Spence decided they better not go back to the cave, but instead they better move on and find Bubba at Shark Hole to see if he found any signs of Drax. By the time they caught up to the guys at Shark Hole it was dusk. It only took a couple of minutes to tell the same story as Bubba. It was getting dark. Spence told the others that they had better get back to the cave before it got too late. They kept to the shoreline, and with the moon out it was easier to see than being in the dense bush. As they got close to Church Bay, Keno was looked across the Sound and saw a light flickering out in the water. Keno stopped, pointed across the Sound and said, "What's that? See that light out in the Sound?"

Everyone looked out and they saw the light too.

Spence replied, "That's a camp fire."

Bubba said, "On the water?"

"No, that's an island out there," replied Spence.

"Look, that sly fox. Drax is out there on the island. He's cut his distance to Shark Hole in half."

Cooter, standing there in amazement said, "With that fire burning out in plain sight he's telling us he could care less if we know he's out there."

"Well look at it from his point of view, if he's on the smallest island, no one's going to surprise him with a sneak attack," replied Spence.

"Well, we just wasted a day looking for Drax and he's right under our noses. I sure hope Michael and Portagee are Ok," Spence continued.

Bubba then added, "Well, they're not going anywhere tonight, let's get back to the cave and see what kind of grub Salty has cooked up for us."

With that they all headed back to the cave very hungry and tired. Upon arriving back at the cave Spence updated the others with the day's events or the non events of the day.

Salty had dinner waiting for the scouting parties, he said, "We didn't wait for you, but I kept your dinner warm anyway. You guys can clean up the mess when you're done, I'm going to bed."

With that, Salty and most of the others went to bed. Tomorrow was another day.

Drax and two of his pirates sat around the fire while the fourth pirate walked around the small island watching for invaders. Each pirate on guard duty had a goat's horn to blow through to warn of danger. The boys were no longer tied back to back to a tree. They were free to walk around; however, Drax insisted their hands remained tied. Michael and Portagee now sat down by the fire to stay warm, as the night had become a little breezy. While they sat there Drax was studying them, and then asked, "You lads sure dress strange? You even talk strange, where are you from?"

Michael replied, "I'm from the United States and Roderick is from Bermuda."

"What's the United Stated?" replied Drax.

Michael was a little surprised at first, then it dawned on him when Drax was in the other world it wasn't the United States.

"You know, the Colonies, we won our independence from Great Britain, the last battle of the war was in 1781", replied Michael.

Drax then looked over at Portagee and said, "And I suppose Bermuda has their independence also?"

"No sir, we're a self governing British Colony."

"So are you two enemies? Since one of you fought the British and one of you are British," Drax asked.

Michael replied, "No sir. We're allies now. In fact, in World War II we fought German Nazis like Stryker."

Drax was getting a little confused now and it was beginning to show in his demeanor.

"You must think I'm stupid. The British and Colonist fighting together, Bull. So when I leave here and head to Boston with my treasure I have to watch out for the colonist too?"

Michael realizing this conversation was going downhill, responded by saying, "Captain Drax sir, the world is very different now, you might not be happy there."

Drax stood up and yelled, "You little bloody brat, your just trying to confuse me with your lies. I should just kill you right now."

He drew his saber out and stuck it on Michael's chest, then said, "You're just a liar. Aren't you?"

Michael swallowed very hard and responded, "Yes sir, sorry sir, please forgive me."

Drax, disgusted, dropped down his saber, reached over and picked up his bottle of rum then walked off. Michael looked over at Portagee, he was still shaking. Portagee told him he did the right thing. With that they both layed down by the fire to go to sleep.

23

SHARKS AT THE GATEWAY

The heavy cool breezes that Michael and Portagee had felt the night before were turning into the makings of a gale force storm by morning. Inspector Savage had been watching the island forecasts religiously for storms of any type. Last night a gale force storm was heading for the island and should be full force by nightfall. He still wasn't one hundred percent sure about storms and opening gateways to the Triangle, but he wasn't going to take any chances with the lives of his daughter and friends. The Inspector had already called Graham to see if he wanted to go with him in the afternoon to "stake out", Shark Hole. Savage knew if the gateway opened in the storm the kids would find themselves in rough waters when they returned. Graham had now shown up at the police station to meet the Inspector, and from there they went down to the harbor police station to check out some equipment. Graham and the Inspector loaded into the squad car, two rubber boats, six twenty five foot ropes, and two large battery powered spot lights and three life preservers. The Inspector was determined to set the stage for a successful rescue if the kids returned that night. The pair left St. George's for Shark Hole, both knowing they would have lots to do that afternoon and the storm would make it even harder to accomplish. The storm was living up to its forecast, as the day went on the storm picked up its velocity. If the gateway needed a strong storm to help open the door, then this was going to blast it wide open. The Inspector and

Graham moved all the supplies and equipment down to a little abandoned house almost on the shoreline next to the Shark Hole. At least there, they had a place to organize and a place to stay somewhat dry. Both the boats were inflated, Ian and Graham then took them with ropes and climbed up to where they were looking down at the entrance to Shark Hole. They attached the ropes to the boats and tossed them down into the water, and then they secured the ropes to trees above the cave. The boats were now floating in place just in front of the cave. Next, they dropped two more ropes down in front of the cave entrance just dangling in the water - these ropes were also tied to trees to anchor them. On each side of the cave on the shoreline they placed the spotlights in the rocks pointing them at the entrance to the cave. Then they took the two life preservers, tied ropes to them, placed them next to the spotlights and also tied these ropes to close by trees. The plan was to stay in the small house until they saw activity in the cave, then they would each take a place by the spotlight and preservers, ready to help the Spinners as they came through the gateway. They now had in place, ropes, boats and preservers, plus lights. The Inspector wanted to make sure no one was swept out into the Sound. The two were ready now and all they could do was to wait the storm out to see what happened. They had no idea that Axle had followed them and he had seen everything that they had done.

Axle had seen enough, he hopped on his scooter and headed back to St. George's in hopes that he would find Tattoo Jack at the Shinbone Pub. As luck would have it, Axle found Tattoo Jack and the other thugs sitting around, drinking as usual. The weather was too nasty to be doing anything on the "Black Shark". Axle told Tattoo Jack what he had seen and that there must be some big event happening that night.

Tattoo stood up and said, "Boys, this may be the big night. The Inspector's gone to a lot of trouble today. The man who recovers my Tucker Cross for me tonight gets $25,000.00."

He now had the attention of the goons. Tonight they would probably kill each other for the chance of getting the cross and that's exactly what Tattoo hoped to accomplish.

He continued, "Tonight there's going to be so much wind and rain, the Inspector will never know we're there until it's too late. Sledge when we get there, I want you to stay up on the road on the east side of the cave, so that you cab be ready to go with the flow and react to the cross. No matter what, you make sure that cross does not get away. Axle, you and Gunner come with me; we'll be above the cave in the rocks waiting to use those ropes the Inspector has most graciously left for us to use. You two wait and do what I tell you to do. Let's get going before something happens before we get there. Because of the terrible weather the trip to Shark Hole was slow. Tattoo had Axle pull the truck over on a side road about a half mile before Shark Hole, and then they would walk the rest of the way. He did not want to take any chances of being seen by the Inspector, or later having his truck being seen close by the cave. Just as Tattoo expected, there was so much commotion going on at Shark Hole they were able to move into their positions without being noticed by Graham or the Inspector.

Now there was the wait. Tattoo's goons were uncomfortable, being soaking wet and cold, but not Tattoo, his dream was about to come true. The Tucker Cross would be his.

Flashing back to the morning, Bubba and Jason were the first out of the cave to observe the bad weather setting in on the island. Jason told Bubba that if this continued, Drax would be heading for Shark Hole sometime during the day. Jason called down into the cave for Keno and Cooter to come up top. When they came up Jason told them to quickly eat their breakfast and take enough food and water to stay out all day, down on the shoreline of the Sound. If they saw Drax or any of his men leaving the island and going in the direction of Shark Hole, before the rest arrived, Keno was to run back to the cave to warn the rest of the group. Cooter and Keno were off to the Sound within an hour, to keep an eye on Drax. The rest of the group got together after breakfast to discuss a strategy to deal with Drax.

Spence spoke up first, "We will only have one chance to stop Drax should the gateway open up. Not only do we have to stop him, we have to save Michael and Portagee. Plus keep the gateway open for the Spinners, so they can enter the gateway and go back to their love ones."

Jason spoke up, "Here's what I think we should do, unless someone objects. Buford and Cooter need to be stationed on the west side of Shark Hole with two muskets apiece. Bubba and Doc need to be stationed on the east side, equipped in the same manner. They would need to keep their gun powder dry and be ready to shoot to kill the pirates on signal. I will then be stationed above the cave with Keno and Sam. I'll slide down a rope and get control of the cross to keep the gateway open, and then Sam and Keno will slide down the rope and hopefully go home. Salty and Georgette will help Doc and Bubba, while Lynn will give Cooter and Buford a hand. Spence, while all this is happening I want you lie low in the rocks, east of the cave, and when all hell breaks loose, I want you to swim over to the last boat, climb in the back of it and take control. The only thing that might change you diving into the water, is if there are sharks swimming around the cave entrance. If there are no questions, then let's all get ready to go."

Drax and his three pirates had been very busy getting the two longboats and the old whaleboat ready for their short one-way trip that evening. The waves in the Sound were already very rough, so Drax loaded the boats on the shore, keeping them out of the water. All three of the boats were tied to each other to make sure they didn't get separated from each other. Drax knew it was critical to keep the boats together and one behind the other as they pass through the narrow gateway. He was also convinced that the Pilgrims would be waiting for him at Shark Hole to try to stop him from going through the gateway. Drax understood human nature and his plan was simple and deadly. He had already made two, six foot ropes with a thirty pound rock on one end and a noose to go around the necks of Michael and Portagee. The Pilgrims would know what was going to happen to the rocks if Drax were to be attacked. He was also going to have razor sharp sabers stuck into the backs of Michael and Portagee when they got close to Shark Hole. They would also have muskets on board; however, he felt that they would not fire because the powder would probably be wet from all of the rain. Each pirate would have their sabers and daggers and would be ready for the unexpected.

As the day went on, just as it had back in the other world, weather conditions continued to get worse. Drax was more elated as the day continued and as the storm grew in strength, he knew this was the key to opening the gateway wide enough to get his boats with the treasure through. He was going to be the king of the high seas. Darkness was setting in, and because of the heavy black clouds it was much darker than it should have been at this time. The water in the Sound was very choppy; it would be difficult at best for the six on board of the three boats to maintain their course to Shark Hole. The boats finally shoved off. Drax knew he would need extra time and that they would have to pace themselves. Michael was in the lead boat with Drax and Portagee was in the second boat. The nooses were already around their necks and they could see the large rock secured to the other end of the rope. Both were thinking what if their boats capsized in this rough water, they would be at the bottom of the Sound very quickly and the pirates would just save themselves. Drax was expecting a hostile reception party when they arrived at the cave, but he just didn't know what they were going to try, to prevent him from entering the gateway.

The Pilgrims and Spinners had just arrived. Spence and Jason were busy reminding everyone where they needed to be. Sam had come up with a good idea to help try to keep the musket's gun powder dry. She had taken her last four plastic head covers and secured them over the hammer and powder hole area on the muskets. Hopefully the muskets would fire when they needed them. Jason did remember to bring the 22 caliber pistol he had rescued off the ship wreck a week or so ago. The problem with the little pistol was that it was only going to work at close range and he had never tried to fire it, so he wasn't even sure it would work. While the others got into place Jason, Keno and Sam secured the ropes to trees just above the cave entrance. Jason knew that when the time arrived he would have one chance to save Michael and Portagee. The rain was almost horizontal now, if it wasn't for the lightening strikes lighting up the blackened skies they would never have be able to see Drax and his boats approaching.

The boats were now within one hundred yards off the Shark Hole entrance, and Drax was at the head of the boat desperately looking for the positions of the Pilgrims. Spotting them was useless, even with the flashes of light from the lightening; it was still too dark up in the rocks and bush to see anyone. They continued to row in the rough waters for another twenty minutes at which point they finally were within twenty yards of the cave entrance. Drax got up and moved behind Michael, he made him stand up then stuck his saber into Michael's back. Two pirates kept rowing the lead boat, which was actually towing the two boats behind it. Portagee was in the second boat and was also standing up, like Michael, with the pirate standing behind him, a dagger stuck into his back. The third boat had no one in it except for the treasure. The lead boat was now within ten yards and Drax was ready to play his hand with the Pilgrims.

He yelled, "Pilgrims, can you hear me, can you hear me?"

Jason responded from up in the rocks with out being seen, "Yes you cutthroat, I hear you."

Drax replied, "Very good mate." He then signaled one of his pirates to lift up a torch that was still barely burning. As he did so, the Pilgrims could see the saber and the dagger being stuck into the backs of Michael and Portagee. They also saw the heavy rope nooses around their necks. Drax continued, "If you try anything your two young friends will have my saber or my mate's dagger thrust through their backs and if that's not enough the other ends of the ropes are connected to large rocks that we will throw overboard and the boys will find themselves at the bottom of the Sound. Do you understand what will happen if you interfere?"

"Yes," replied Jason.

The lead boat was within five yards of the cave and the storm now seemed to be at its peak. Drax now pulled the cross out of his old tattered coat, held it over the shoulder of Michael, and very quickly the emeralds in the cross started pulling the power of the storm, casting it's brilliant triangular beam into the cave entrance. Sparks, beams and green electromagnetic waves began emitting from the cave. Drax starting shaking from all the intensity of the opposing forces being created. He had felt this before and knew not to let go.

The Inspector and Graham, although on opposite sides of the cave were now seeing the Sparks and beams and green electromagnetic waves emitting from deep within the cave from both sides.

Graham yelled over at the Inspector, "It's starting; something is going to happen tonight."

Tattoo heard what Graham had said and thought to himself, "Your right, I'm going to happen tonight and get my cross back".

Drax's boat was now almost to the entrance of the cave and Jason knew this was the time to make his move. He grabbed one of the ropes with both hands and jumped off the ledge over the entrance of the cave. He swung down just in front of Michael and grabbed the cross out of Drax's hand as he went by. He then pushed off the side of the cave and looped back around Drax and dropped to the back of the boat. The gateway had just begun to open and now had shut back down. Drax still had his arm around

Michael. Jason was slightly stunned from his fall, and before he could recover, the two pirates dropped their oars and began to attack Jason. Jason quickly pulled out his pistol and fired two shots each into the two pirates. Being within two to three feet of them the shots were effective. One pirate fell dead into the water and the other dropped down on his boats bench mortally wounded. Drax seeing what was happening, was slightly stunned as he had never seen a pistol that could shoot more than one shot.

Drax yelled out, "Throw the Portuguese boy over board, you'll pay for this Pilgrims."

Jason screamed, "No, don't do it." But it was too late. The pirate holding Portagee reached down, picked up the heavy rock and threw it into the Sound. Portagee was with in a second snapped off the boat and into the Sound.

Portagee's friends on the shore were stunned; they were standing there in shock. Spence however, quickly reacted and dove into the water after Portagee. The water was pitch black with only glimmers of light from the lightening above the Sound. Portagee hit bottom and struggled to get loose but the knot was stitched closed, making it impossible to loosen. With the blood in the water from the dead pirate, sharks were now also a threat. Spence swam in the direction where he saw Portagee fall into the water. He was swimming blindly.

Spence went deeper, starting to panic a little not finding Portagee, then about twenty feet away he saw something metal flashing when the lightening bolts flashed. He swam faster toward the reflections, it was Portagee, and he had seen his Spinners keychain spinning in the water. When he got to Portagee he tapped him on the shoulder to get to stop struggling and save his air supply. Portagee stopped, Spence quickly drew out his dagger and started cutting at the knot in the noose. Within twenty seconds he had it cut apart. Spence signaled Portagee to follow him. He did. They surfaced just behind the third boat, both stayed just out of sight and hung on to the back of the boat. They would crawl into the back of the boat when they were sure they were not being watched.

Meanwhile Jason stood up and threaten, "You murderer, I'll kill you Drax."

Drax laughed, keeping the saber in the back of Michael, he turned to Jason and said, "You better drop the pistol or my man will thrust his saber through your back and I'll kill this boy, just like we killed the other one."

Jason dropped the pistol.

Drax then said, "Good, now hold that cross up and in the direction of the cave if you want the boy to live."

Bubba and the others on the shore with the muskets were forced to wait and see, they could not take any chances with Michael's life. Jason meanwhile raised the cross in the direction of the cave and the brilliance of the emeralds began to affect the gateway again.

Drax then said, "That's very good Pilgrim, drop that cross and you're a dead man." The pirate with the saber reminded Jason he was behind him, therefore Jason could do nothing but comply. Now that the focus of attention was on the entrance to the cave, Spence helped Portagee crawl into the boat and hide behind the treasure chest. Spence followed directly behind him, not a moment too soon, as sharks had began ripping apart the dead pirate.

The gateway was now opening much wider. Drax's boat is now slowly drawn into the cave by the force of the gateway.

The other side the gateway has finally opened and the Inspector and Graham can see glimmers of images moving on the other side of the gateway.

Graham yells out, "Look the gateway is opening Inspector. I can see reflections of people and look the beams from the cross can be seen."

The Inspector can't believe his eyes - this is really happening - the Bermuda Triangle is opening up right before his eyes. Tattoo heard Graham's comments and he knew it was just about time to make his play for the cross. He stood up, went to the edge of the ledge and quickly began pulling up the rope. The Inspector notices the movement of the rope and looked up to see Tattoo. He then warned Tattoo, "You stay out of this Skinner, and this has nothing to do with you."

Tattoo replied, "On the contrary Inspector, there's a possession of mine in there and I intend to go and get it."

With that Tattoo took the rope, jumped off the ledge and swung into the cave. As he reached the gateway, he let go of the rope and yelled, "Look out devil, her I come."

His body flew through the gateway causing electromagnetic explosions and green lightening blasting in all directions. The blast blew outwards towards the boats trying to enter the gateway from the other side. Jason could see a body flying through the air in the gateway on a collision coarse with Michael.

Jason yelled, "Michael drop quickly, get out of the way."

At that split second Michael dropped to his knees, Tattoo came flying through the gateway, sailing over Michael and before Drax could move Tattoo was impaled on his saber. At that same moment the pirate drew back his saber to run it through Jason, but before he could do that Spence jumped up from behind the treasure chest and threw his dagger into the back of the pirate. The pirate's body jerked and then fell over into the Sound. Tattoo lived long enough to see Jason holding the cross. His body was hanging over Drax, with his right hand he reached for the cross, and then died.

Drax then pulled his saber out of Tattoo and turned to kill Jason. From both sides of the shore line all four muskets fired on Drax causing him to instantly drop in the water, and within seconds you could hear Drax screaming as the sharks attacked him.

The gateway was now fully opened and you could see clearly from both sides. Michael waved to Graham and the Inspector. Sam and Keno now slid down the ropes into the boat. Portagee and Spence moved forward from the back boat to the front boat. Jason and Spence hugged the Spinners, knowing it was time for them to go home.

Keno, with tears in his eyes said, "I can't leave I belong here."

Michael added, "So do I."

Jason and Spence were very surprised by the comments of Keno and Michael. Jason responded, "That's a noble thought, but your lives are ahead of you, you need to go home to your families. When you finish your schooling and become adults, then you can make the decision to come back here. We'll welcome you back. For now though, your families are waiting for you, please go. We'll all miss you."

Sam came forward and added, "Take these phones and keep the cross, you know how to contact us. By you keeping the cross you will control the gateway. When we go back home we will make sure this gateway is protected."

With that the storm was slowly dying down so the Spinners quickly said their goodbyes. The final gesture came when Portagee pulled out his Spinner keychain and gave it to Jason, but only after he received a nod of approval from Michael, then Sam and Keno gave theirs to Jason also, Portagee then looked down and saw his Spinner key-chain on the floor of the boat, Tattoo must have dropped it when he died. Portagee then picked it up and handed his to Spence. Michael then said, "This is all we have to give you, to us it's more than just a keychain it represents our bond to each other, we want you to have these as a token of our appreciation". Jason shook Michaels hand and then said, "We will always honor your gift & will never forget you". Sam added, "You all are truly the Protectors of the Triangle".

While all this was going on, they were being watched by someone in the bushes. Bubba just happen to look over and see the blinking demonic eye for a split second, and then it was gone.

Spence then said, "You better get going while you can. Come on Jason we need to climb these ropes and let our friends go home."

With that they grabbed the ropes, Spence climbed on up the rope while Jason clung to the rope, but kept the cross focused on the cave to make sure the gateway remained open until the Spinners passed through. As the three boats passed through the gateway there were electromagnetic explosions and green lightening blasting in all directions. The blast blew outwards towards the Inspector and Graham, almost knocking them off their feet. They recovered to watch the three boats emerged from the cave. Michael stood up in the boat and threw a rope to the Inspector, who then pulled the boats to the shore. Tattoo's men realizing that Tattoo was not coming back, decided it was a good time to flee before the Inspector could see them. By the time the boats were tied up, the gateway had closed. Sam jumped out of the boat and ran over to her father and hugged him. Graham quickly got over to the side of the cave where the boats were tied up, and he then hugged everyone in sight.

While the Inspector received an update from everyone, Graham called the parents of Keno, Portagee and Michael's grandmother to come and meet them. When Graham finished making his calls, he walked over to the boats, noticing the chests in each of them. He asked Portagee what was in them. They had all forgotten about the boats.

Portagee then said to Graham, "Oh, it's just treasure."

Graham and Portagee then jumped into one of the boats and broke open one of the chests.

"Holy Cow," Graham screamed. The Inspector and others came over to look at the chest.

The Inspector, in disbelief said, "The treasure in this chest alone must be worth over a million dollars and this is only one chest out of twenty on these boats."

The Spinners all looked at the Inspector, with Sam speaking for them, "Father, we all want to take some of the money from this treasure and protect this gateway forever, so our friends on the inside of the Triangle can use it when needed and we may visit them from time to time."

The Inspector replied, "You can count on me kids. Tomorrow we will all meet with Graham's father and he will help us develop a Trust to protect this site forever."

The Spinners all hugged the Inspector again, and by now the parents were beginning to show up. The Inspector called for a Police paddy wagon to come to pick up the treasure chests to keep them safe until the dust had settled. He didn't want to take any chances in case Skinner's men were still lurking around. After about two hours the family reunions had been made and the treasure was safely off to the police department in St. George's.

24

PROTECTORS OF THE TRIANGLE

Several months had passed since the Spinners had returned from the Triangle. The Inspector and Mr. Aston, Graham's father, lived up to their promises to protect the gateway to the Triangle. The treasure had been valued at over thirty million dollars, with the explanation of the find, that Hurricane Fabian had uncovered the buried treasure from the bottom of Harrington Sound and the kids had stumbled onto it snorkeling. Fortunately, the Inspector never had to swear in a court of law what happened. After the split with the Bermuda government the Spinners still had over fifteen million dollars. Mr. Aston used his influence to establish a Trust called "Spinners Trust", with its sole purpose to protect one of Bermuda's natural resources. The Trust donated one million dollars to the Bermuda Government; in return they would receive a two hundred year lease on Shark Hole. The outside of the cave would remain untouched. About midway into the cave there was installed an indestructible non metallic two inch bar fence with a gate. Being non metallic the fence would not interfere with the gateway and the electromagnetic waves. Only the Spinners & their friends in the Triangle, knew the touchpad combination to the lock on the gate. Portagee, being the electronic whiz kid that he was developed a new GPS device for their friends to communicate with the Spinners. These new devices are about the size of a dollar coin, the bottom of the device is rubber, making them floatable and they have five preprogrammed buttons on the top of it. They would simply press the button with the preprogrammed message in it and then sent it through the gateway. Once back in Bermuda it would transmit the message to all of the Spinners' cell phones plus to a computer at the new Spinner's Trust office in St. Georges. The Spinner GPS device would render itself useless five hours after it transmitted, so there was no reason to recover it unless it had a note attached to it. The messages were simple, need medical supplies, need other supplies, need to make contact – read note attached, no contact needed this month and have visitors to return. It was agreed that a GPS device would be sent out once a month from the Triangle to the Spinners.

The Pilgrims, without the threat of the Nazis and Drax and his pirates, felt it was time to move to a new home on the island. They moved to the location where Drax had his encampment in St. Georges. This location had much better natural resources, better lookout posts, many huts and facilities that had been there for years. Salty was back home in his hut he called the galley, Doc finally had his little infirmary. Last but not least, there was still millions of dollars worth of treasure that Drax had left behind in his hast to leave the Triangle.

The Pilgrims as always were ready to help other lost souls to survive in the Triangle when they arrived. They were also on a constant state of alert to protect the island from future evil intruders who enter the Triangle with destruction in mind.

Spence, Jason and the others all wondered which of the Spinners would be the first ones to come back.

Only time would tell...And they had all the time in the world.

SPINNERS BERMUDA MAP INDEX:

MAP ON BACK COVER

1) Battle of St. Georges, Bartram Island
2) Pirate Lookout Post, Fort George Hill
3) Wreck "Typhoon"
4) Unfinished Cathedral
5) St. George's Island
6) Pirate Encampment
7) Convict Bay
8) Gates Bay
9) St. David's Lighthouse
10) Howard Bay
11) Shark Hole
12) Crystal Caves
13) Church Bay
14) Coney Island
15) Crow Island
16) The Devils Hole
17) John Smith's Bay
18) Tuckers Bay
19) Flatts Inlet, Aquarium Museum and Zoo
20) Gibbons Bay
21) Pilgrim Settlement, Admiralty House Park
22) Clarence Cove
23) Hinson Island
24) Soncy Cove
25) Saltus Island
26) Somerset Island
27) Watford Island
28) Boaz Island
29) Ireland Island South
30) Ireland Island North
31) Nazi Encampment, Royal Naval Dockyard